Thank you Jeff Vande Zande for creating Denver Hoptner and returning him home for a Saginaw summer to be transformed by its malleable iron heat.

Forged in personal crisis, Denver loved and hated his hometown as he walked its tension-filled streets where he felt his poetic voice unwelcome, another lost son, much like Roethke two generations before.

Denver was stuck in writer's block, a writer who couldn't write, until he learned that it was because of Saginaw that Roethke found his images to write. Until he learned to go back to move forward and take a second look to discover new perspectives, until he valued his father's teachings of history of place and of hard work, not taking the easy way but do it right, only then was he able to discover his own uniqueness and potential in the context of his community and begin to answer ancient life questions: Who am I? What do I have to give?

Denver's 'rite of passage' so filled with courage, sacrifice and risk guides us in what's important. May more of us listen to his shouts of "Save this House" to serve Roethke's hometown and to honor a poet's life. May more of us climb with Denver and Jeff Vande Zande to become 'children on top of the greenhouse.' Let's have it crowded up there!

–Annie Ransford, president Friends of Theodore Roethke

Other books by Jeff Vande Zande:

Fiction:
Emergency Stopping and Other Stories (Bottom Dog Press)
Into the Desperate Country: a novel (March Street Press)
Landscape with Fragmented Figures: a novel (Bottom Dog Press)
Threatened Species and Other Stories (Whistling Shade Press)

Poetry:
Poems New, Used, and Rebuilds (March Street Press)

Anthologies Edited:
On the Clock: Contemporary Short Stories of Work (Bottom Dog Press)

AMERICAN POET

A NOVEL

JEFF VANDE ZANDE

WORKING LIVES SERIES
BOTTOM DOG PRESS

HURON, OHIO

CREDITS:
General Editor: Larry Smith
Layout & Design: Susanna Sharp-Schwacke
Cover Design: Susanna Sharp-Schwacke and Larry Smith
Cover Art: Jennifer Vande Zande
Author Photograph: Jennifer Vande Zande

ACKNOWLEDGMENTS
A special thanks goes to the editors at Central Michigan University's *Temenos* magazine for publishing an excerpt from *American Poet* in their *Low Over Gratiot*, a special Roethke edition of their journal. I also thank The Friends of Theodore Roethke for giving me a tour of Theodore Roethke's boyhood home, and for allowing me to spend a night there to work on the novel.

Thanks to JodiAnn Stevenson for being an early reader of the book and making me believe that I was onto something.

Thanks also to JodiAnn Stevenson for allowing me to excerpt her poem "God Is In What Is Not Made," which appears in its full form in her chapbook, *Diving Headlong Into a Cliff of Our Own Delusion* (Saucebox Books).

Special appreciation to Gina Myers for closely reading a later version of the book. This book wouldn't be what it is without her careful line editing.

Additionally, I thank H.J Gornowicz for the use of his poem, "Thanksgiving Eve."

The following books were invaluable when it came to the writing of *American Poet*:

The Glass House: The Life of Theodore Roethke by Allan Seager (University of Michigan Press)

And *d.a. levy and the mimeograph revolution* (Bottom Dog Press)

Finally, thank you to Larry Smith for being such a good steward while being my editor and publisher for this book.

you can watch the ones who
didnt move fast enough
they are dying
& they are called poets
                    —d.a. levy, American Poet

"I am the world crier, and this is my dangerous career. I am the
one to call your bluff."
                    —Kenneth Patchen, American Poet

I wake to sleep, and take my waking slow.
I feel my fate in what I cannot fear.
I learn by going where I have to go.
                    — Theodore Roethke, American Poet

1.

The summer was going to end with God and the fall and pink rabbit light. In May, though, zipping my jacket against the cold, the only thing I knew was that I'd been back in Saginaw living in my dad's house for almost a month. It seemed like a year. To keep from going nuts, I went for walks almost every night. I'd just graduated from college, but felt like a teenager again. Dad had nothing but questions. He wanted to know where I was going at night. He wanted to know what my plans were for the day. If I was in the room, he studied me, like somebody surveying a stagnant pond for signs of life. His eyes seemed to ask, just when the hell was this kid going to get up and do something productive?

I shivered, looking at the faint light bleeding through the drawn blinds of the houses around me.

I couldn't find decent work in Ann Arbor, and none of the grad schools had offered me a teaching assistantship, which pretty much meant that I wasn't going. With no job in A², living with my dad for awhile seemed like a way to regroup and consider my options.

Bad idea.

My mom had died the summer before, and Dad and I really didn't get along. She'd been the cartilage between us, keeping us from banging head-on into each other, or grinding one another down into splinters. Turns out we weren't much good to each other without her.

I jammed my hands into my pockets. I had taken Malzahn to where it became Wheeler St. and knew that if I followed it a little farther it would take me to Gratiot. From there I could find Theodore Roethke's boyhood home. It was one of the few things that I didn't hate about the town. When I was in high school and thinking that maybe I wanted to write, I used to walk out to the Roethke House at least once a month, just to look at it. He was a pretty big poet in his day. Pulitzer Prize for one thing, and it meant something that a guy like that could come from a place like Saginaw. He was a guide.

A lodestar.

I'd gotten it in my head to sneak behind the Roethke place to see the greenhouses. During class one night, Professor Seager had a Roethke poem on a transparency and projected it on the screen behind him. It wasn't very long, titled "Child on Top of a Greenhouse." It described a little Teddy Roethke up on the glass top of a greenhouse in high winds and all the adults pointing up at him and shouting.

"That's about more than some child," Seager said, pointing at the screen and then at us. "That little boy...that's symbolic of Roethke's poet soul." He tapped his finger at his heart. "All poets, if they're any good, come at the world like children. Full of wonder but, above all, curious...deadly curious, and mischievous.

"They scramble up to dangerous heights. They have to, you know? Just to look around, to get a different perspective. At the risk of falling, they show us what we sometimes refuse to see. Even when everybody is shouting them down."

Seager pointed at the air above our heads. He'd get really worked up in class. He was good, one of my favorites. "If you have the poet's soul, you can't help but climb. The hell with high winds and the 'elms plunging and tossing like horses.' It is your burden to climb. That poem is Roethke recognizing it in himself, the dual nature of the poet's soul. Afraid to fall and yet more afraid of not climbing."

Despite the chilled air, I trudged on. I wanted to see where Roethke had climbed, and maybe even climb up there myself.

Something.

I crossed Ottawa Street. Another Algonquin Indian word. The town was littered with them.

My old man had told me about the Sauks, an Indian tribe that lived in the Saginaw Valley hundreds of years ago...here before any of it. Before the fur traders, before the lumberjacks and the sugar beet farmers, or the rise and fall of the auto industry. The Sauks had it good, back when the Saginaw River bed wasn't laced with dioxins. There were huge pines everywhere.

"They had it so good," Dad said, "that the Chippewas, the Hurons, the Pottawatamies, and the Menominees started paying attention."

The four tribes held a council on an island in the Straits of Mackinaw. They decided to relieve the Sauks of the burden of hunting and fishing all that land and water. Coming into the Saginaw Bay by canoe and up the river, or coming by land through the forest, they surrounded the unsuspecting Sauks. Hidden in the darkness of the trees, they must have watched the clearing—the fire, the dancing—like something out of Plato's Cave. "They listened to the singing," Dad said. "Then, under a bright moon, they gave a signal." The four tribes fell upon the Sauks while they were holding a harvest festival in honor of a young chief named Raven's Eye. Raven's Eye—that name had always stayed with me.

The Sauks were slaughtered and their land taken. "None of them survived," Dad had said, looking into my eyes.

Raven's Eye. Young. Probably optimistic. He never could have guessed that everything was going to go to shit. How is it that things turn out the way they do? Watching his people running, getting butchered around him, he must have been thinking about how the day had started in such promise. They were going to have this festival. They were going to celebrate a good harvest.

Then everything fell apart.

That's the way it was with my own life. With trying to write poems. With Heather. With my grad school applications. Even with the position at the library over in Midland. When they sent me the letter telling me that they'd filled the part-time librarian position, I called the director to find out why I hadn't even been interviewed. She told me that they were looking for somebody with a Library Science degree. It wasn't enough that I loved books. It wasn't enough that I had a degree from the University of Michigan. No, I had to be a damn scientist. She didn't even laugh when I told her that I could probably get my hands on a lab coat and fake the rest.

I sat for awhile listening to the dial tone after she hung up. "Kiss my ass," I whispered to the echoing hum on the other end. I'd more or less guaranteed my dad that the position would be mine. After it fell through, he started offering advice about jobs and possible leads. I started taking more walks.

Somebody yelled "faggot" from a car window at me, sending adrenaline jumping up my spine. I shook my head, glaring at the taillights.

Jesus, this place.

The name of this half-dead city: Saginaw, an Algonquin word that means "the place of the Sauks." Fitting, really. Place of the dead. Place of the slaughtered. Place of the forgotten. It's a city made for ghosts.

Roethke was a ghost, too. A weedy ghost that barely even haunted the place.

When I was a senior in high school, there was a festival in celebration of Roethke's birthday. They brought in a big poet from Michigan State University for a reading. I'd gone, expecting hundreds to be out celebrating the city's greatest poetic son. There were less than thirty people. Even fewer stayed to hear the poet from MSU. It was just

9

as well. I didn't understand any of his poems. I didn't go on the tour of the inside of the house, but I did take the shuttle out to Roethke's grave at Oakwood Cemetery. A handful of people were there to read four or five of his poems aloud. It actually felt like a funeral.

They shouldn't have called it a festival.

It was really cold, more like March than May. I flexed my fingers in my pockets and flipped my sweatshirt hood up, huddling into myself. Televisions flickered grey light in the front windows of homes. I was alone except for the taillights and headlights sliding past. It was this cold back in November when Heather had told me that things weren't working out between us. "It's not that I don't love you," she'd started to say. I just walked away. I knew the rest. She was going to tell me that she loved me as a friend.

She'd called just the night before to tell me that she'd already written three new poems. I sat stone-faced on a bed in my father's basement, my feet cold on the concrete, listening to her. She'd been accepted to spend a week at Fallingbrook, some writer's retreat in upstate New York. They waived half her tuition fee because of the "promise of the poems" in her application packet. "These new poems I've got going now…I don't know, they're pretty experimental. New territory for me," she said.

That was a big word with her over the past year—experimental. I never understood it. Trying to create anything is an experiment. Calling it experimental seemed redundant. Of course, most of my words just sat on the page, never making any kind of chemical reaction. What the hell did I know? Heather was the poet. She was the one getting accepted to prestigious writer's retreats. I couldn't get anything to happen. I hadn't written anything all winter, but hoped spring would make a difference.

It didn't.

Heather was meeting a lot of up-and-coming poets and had, just the night before, listened to both Ben Rousseau and Elissa Gotti read as a part of Fallingbrook's weekly Writers-to-Watch Reading Series. I hadn't heard of either of them. I didn't tell her that, but the way she said their names, I thought she suspected as much.

"Rousseau's poems were so beautiful," she said. "I was sitting there just crying." She explained that later in the night Rousseau got drunk and punched out some high school kid that was bussing tables at a Big Boy restaurant. She hadn't heard yet if the kid was going to press charges, but Rousseau was in jail, that much she knew. All of his talks and seminars at Fallingbrook had been canceled.

"Sounds like an asshole," I said.

10

"I don't know, you would have had to hear his poems. I think he's pretty tortured inside with a pretty messed up past."

I picked up on her subtext. She was telling me that I hadn't been there, that I was out of the loop. I didn't know Rousseau, the man. But, then, how could I? I wasn't at Fallingbrook. I didn't hear his poems. I would probably never hear his poems. That being the case, I was in no position to pass judgment, even on something as cut and dry as a grown man—an assistant professor at Idaho State—decking some skinny, seventeen-year-old kid holding a tub load of dirty plates and silverware.

The poetry world—the real poetry world outside of U of M—was a larger mystery. I was uninitiated, and she was trying to explain, in the simplest way possible, the facts as she knew them. And, she always seemed to be making it clear that she knew the facts. She was in the poetry world. She was meeting people with names. It wouldn't be long before she had a name. "I am in," she seemed to be telling me, "and you, Denver Hoptner, are not."

Even so, it was always good to hear her voice. Plus, she had called me. That's what I kept telling myself. She called me. It made me think that there might still be a chance. So why was I being so pathetic about it?

When I finally reached Gratiot St., the traffic was too heavy to try to cross. I turned down the sidewalk, waiting for a lull. I was shivering.

Two days before, when the weather had finally climbed into the fifties, I rode my bike to Old Town Saginaw, the only part of the city that still felt somewhat alive. There were young people. Starry-eyed high school girls. Hipsters. Potheads. Small-town messiahs. There were a few struggling galleries, a few decent restaurants, four or five good bars. I talked to the owner of a coffee shop down there and got him to agree to let me host an open mic poetry night in his place. I had a microphone and amplifier at my father's, left over from high school when I was writing songs and thought I might be a singer, which I wasn't.

Bruce, the owner of the coffee shop, kept bringing the conversation back to making money. He even talked about charging people to read. He shrugged a palm into the air in front of him. "Only like fifty cents a poem or something," he said. I managed to talk him out of that idea. I could tell he was going to be a hassle. Still, I wanted to do something.

I kicked a rock down the sidewalk, trying to keep my mind off the cold. I kept it going for awhile and then lost it in the dark. I tried not to dwell on it.

I'd been thinking a lot about d.a. levy, this Ohio poet and another ghost haunting me. I'd written a paper about him for a class during my last semester, right after Heather dumped me. I'd bought a slim book of his poems from a rare book dealer online. *Cleveland Undercovers and Other Poems*. It cost me fifty bucks. My dad never would have understood that one—fifty bucks pissed away as far as he would be concerned. I'd been carrying the book around in my back pocket every day since moving back home.

levy rained poetry on drought-plagued Cleveland. He started his own mimeograph press and handed out broadsides in the streets. He published all kinds of renegade poets who might not otherwise have been in print. When he saw the same thing going on in New York, he started hosting readings all around Cleveland.

The thing is he also kept a .22 rifle on his wall and threatened to kill himself if he ever started writing bad poems. He wrote against the city's corruption and in spite of their censorship. He didn't write what he thought might get published in some in-crowd 'zine. He wrote what he wanted to write—what he thought needed to be written. He was arrested for reading aloud and publishing poems that others called obscene. Police would show up at his poetry readings. The fucking police.

Crazy.

Poetry wasn't in classrooms for levy. It wasn't a scene or something to brag about on *fucking* Facebook. A poet wasn't something one became by getting a degree. levy didn't trust the things you could gain from institutions. Poetry wasn't at writing retreats or in university journals. It was on the streets. It kicked people in the head and got them to listen. It got people mad and made some afraid—afraid of what poetry could do.

Poetry got people arrested.

levy made it seem like poetry could actually do something, besides build someone's résumé on their way toward landing a cushy university Creative Writing position.

levy lived big. And then he didn't.

At twenty-six years old, he gave nearly everything away over the course of a few weeks. In 1968, alone in his apartment, he took down that .22 rifle, propped it between his legs, and shot himself in the forehead. Twenty-six years old. Things must have felt pretty damn bleak.

The first poem I discovered on my own was one of levy's. It was beautiful:

> when riding the winter pony
> one

leaves
a trail of bells
softly ringing
deep in the mind
& if one listens
perhaps the sound
will guide
             the young rider through the
falling
snow

I don't know...something about that poem. I read it until I could finally make some kind of meaning from it. I didn't want a professor to tell me what it meant. I didn't need that. I could do it on my own. That winter pony. It is life. And death. We're riding, but the pony is taking us into winter. Life leads us step by step to death. It's going to happen. What can we do about it? levy was saying that we have to listen. Not to the shit, all that noise out there...all the crap. We have to listen for the quiet stuff underneath all the static...those softly ringing bells, man. That's the stuff poetry can help us hear. The snow is falling—it's always falling—and listening closely can make the ride a little less cold.

That's what I thought poetry should do, wake people up to that trail of softly ringing bells. levy, though, he kept it real. He didn't romanticize anything or say it would be easy. He said "perhaps"...perhaps if we listen we'll get through all that falling snow.

Perhaps.

Maybe we won't. Maybe some of us just get buried, like levy. The city of Cleveland—the authorities and their police—raged a blizzard at him. It was too much. Too much suffocating snow. They locked him up and shut him down. Shot him down. It was just as much them pulling that trigger as it was him.

Anyway, that's what I was thinking when I looked across the street at the Roethke houses. They were there, looming with dark windows. No lights. On the left, Carl Roethke's big fieldstone. On the right, Otto's hulking white house—the place where Theodore grew up.

Looking at it, though, something wasn't right, something strange on the porch. Yellow. If they were decorations, someone had done a pretty bad job.

A break came in the traffic, and I ran across the street and up into the yard to take a look.

13

Police tape.

The Roethke porch was criss-crossed in police tape.

I just stared for awhile before walking a full circle around the place. I couldn't see anything obvious. No kicked in doors or broken-out basement windows. I came back around to the front yard. It always struck me that the house was just like the man, a hunched gloominess.

I walked up to the porch. The windows were just black squares reflecting the street lights of Gratiot. They told me nothing.

Climbing the steps, I lifted the police tape and dipped myself under it. I cupped my hands around my eyes and leaned down, pressing my vision to one of the windows. The glass was cold on the soft of my palms. I couldn't see much until my eyes started to adjust. A flight of stairs in the shadows off to the left. In the room in front of me, the outline of a piano against the wall.

The window flared with light.

I jumped up and turned around. A car had pulled into the two-rut path across the front lawn that passed for a driveway.

A second later I had to shield my eyes against the spotlight on me. Cops. My heart started banging around in my chest, and I had the sudden urge to piss.

The officer's voice came over his PA. "Come down from there and over to the car," he said. "Now."

I nodded docilely and then scooted back under the tape and down the steps. He kept the light on me as I walked toward the car, squinting. My mouth had gone dry.

When he talked to me again, it was through his rolled down window. I was blind in the glare. "What are you doing here? You can't be up there like that."

A dispatcher on his radio squawked something that I couldn't understand. The heat in my wrists was echoed in the heat behind my ears. His light was still on me like some giant interrogation lamp. "I was just walking by," I said, stammering. "I saw the tape. I was wondering what happened."

I could feel him studying me, looking me up and down. Arms crossed over my chest, I looked at the ground. I couldn't escape the awful blazing light. "This is Theodore Roethke's house," I said, staring into the dirt. "The poet. I just thought maybe I could see what had happened."

He turned off the light. Everything went instantly black, leaving me just as blind.

"They had a fire," he said. "Let me see your i.d."

I slipped my hand into my back pocket for my wallet. I was lucky that I'd taken it with me. Usually I didn't, seeing as how it was almost always empty. Wrestling it out of its plastic sheath, I handed my license over to his waiting palm.

Just a shadow in the car, he shined a small flashlight onto my picture. He studied it for a minute and then punched something into his computer.

"This is expired," he said, like he was accusing me of something.

I swallowed. "I don't drive. I don't have a car." I ran my sweaty fingers through my hair. "If I get a car this summer, I'm going to renew it...I mean, I'll have to, right?"

He asked me where I lived. I told him. I wondered if maybe the fire had been arson. Maybe he thought I was the arsonist returning to see my handiwork. I remembered from Psych class that arsonists often return to the scene of the fire.

I rubbed a finger into the corner of my eye. "I just got back from school down in Ann Arbor. I just graduated. I'm back living with my dad for—"

"You know that was illegal, right? Crossing police tape like you did is a punishable offense."

The back of my neck felt like it was on fire. His face was shadows and little flickers of flesh. "I'm really sorry, officer. I only wanted to know what happened with the house. I mean, it's just that this house...I mean, I'm a really big fan of Roethke's poems—"

"Consider this a warning."

I nodded. "Yes, sir. I'm really sorry. It was stupid—"

"Where are you going from here?"

"Home, sir. Straight home. I told my dad I'd be back before eleven."

He studied me before handing my license back through the window. "Get going, then. You've got some walking ahead of you."

I took the license and stuffed it into my wallet. "Yes, sir. Thank you, sir." He could have said anything, and I would have agreed with him. I started toward the sidewalk.

"Denver," he said. "I don't want to see you around here again."

I stopped and shook my head. "You won't."

I looked back at his taillights a few times as I made my way toward Wheeler. He idled for awhile in Roethke's front yard, probably filling out some kind of report. My heartbeat settled. Then, I started to get angry. The conversation between me and the cop kept replaying in my head. I didn't like the way he said the things he did. What had I done other than be curious? I saw police tape on the Roethke House,

15

and I wanted to know what was going on. Big deal. That house belonged to the community. Police tape didn't change that. He talked to me like he owned the house, like he owned me.

I kept looking back. I was just as angry with myself. Christ, I'd practically licked his boots. Yes, sir. Thank you, sir.

I was blocks away when he finally backed out, and my heart raced a little bit when he came in my direction, headlights bearing down. His face was locked forward as he drove past, like I wasn't even worth a glance.

When he was a good block away, I flipped him the bird.

His taillights kept going, shrinking into the distance and blending in with the rest.

"Kiss my ass," I said. To him. To my dad. To Heather. To everything.

In some way, probably to myself.

2.

The branch manager leaned back in his chair with my résumé, tapping a pencil against the edge of the paper like he was trying to imitate a hummingbird's heartbeat. His eyes scanned around the page, stopped briefly, and then scanned again. He must have been looking for something and was having trouble finding it. He seemed unimpressed.

He lowered the paper and looked at me. He had perfectly squared fingernails. One eye squinted. "It's Denver Hoptner?"

"Hop-ner," I said, glancing at a silhouette passing on the other side of the blinds behind him. "The t is silent."

He nodded his head and smiled, unfazed by my correction. "Unusual first name."

I heard myself say what I'd been saying all of my life: "John Denver was my mom's favorite singer." More than a few times, hearing my explanation, people would break into an impromptu excerpt from "Country Roads" or "Rocky Mountain High" or, my least favorite, "Thank God I'm a Country Boy." I wasn't surprised, though, that the branch manager didn't sing. He didn't seem like the type to much care for lyrics. Or songs. Or anything not directly related to CD rates and ATM fees. He just smiled dismissively, nodded, and then dropped his attention back to my résumé. He was still looking for something...some explanation as to just why in the hell he and I were sitting there in his office.

When I had come in and sat down across from him, he reached over the desk, shook my hand, and apologized right away for the lighting, which amounted to the natural light bleeding in through floor-to-ceiling Venetian blinds on two of the walls. He smiled. "The bank practices sustainability," he said, like it was a selling point, a reason to want the job—a job I think we both pretty much knew he wasn't going to offer me.

His spartan office made me think of *Walden*. His desk was spotless except for a telephone, a keyboard, and a flat-screen monitor. The walls were white and the carpet beige. The room's only painting, an abstract thing, featured a dark blue square dwarfing and overlapping a baby blue square. Pretty simple. Still, if it was simplicity, it wasn't a simplicity that Thoreau would have admired. It was no place to live deliberately. It was a monetary monastery with nothing to distract a branch manager from his business of meditating on the mysteries of money. As far as I was concerned, it was hell and, sadly, a hell I was trying to get checked in to. It was the first interview I'd had in awhile, yet more than anything I just wanted to stand and walk out.

I imagined what my father would think of a move like that. He'd be disappointed, but in no way surprised.

I had called the city about the Roethke House. They couldn't tell me much other than what I already knew—that there had been a fire. After I'd been transferred around a few times, one of the secretaries gave me the phone number for Abby Waters, the President of the Patrons of Roethke, who was more than willing to talk. She talked as though nobody ever asked her enough about the Roethke House.

From what the insurance investigators could tell, squirrels or mice had chewed through the wiring in the attic, which caused an electrical fire. Someone in the neighborhood saw the smoke pretty early on, and the fire department was able to keep things from getting out of control. Still, they ended up with a hole in the roof, fire and water damage to the attic, smoke and water damage to the second floor, and water damage to the first floor. The estimated damages came in at around $75,000. Short of a two thousand dollar deductible, insurance was going to cover it.

When I made a noise that suggested that I was relieved, she told me that they didn't even have the two thousand dollars. She practically told me the entire history of the place. When the house went up for sale in the late nineties, Abby bought it, assuming that the Patrons of Roethke would soon raise the money to buy it from her. "In the early days," she said, "the talk was of restoring the place then buying Carl Roethke's house next door and restoring that, too." Money was the problem. Most years it trickled. "Some years I had to pay out of my own pocket for basic upkeep," she said. The talk of doing anything significant among the Patrons of Roethke soon died down.

"Simply put," she said, "I'm having a hard time even raising the money for the deductible. Some members of the board are starting to talk in terms of lost causes."

I asked her what that meant.

"I don't know. Right now, it means we have a makeshift roof of tarps and a damaged interior that isn't getting better on its own. The mood here is grim. I talk of fund raisers, and I'm met with cynicism and despair."

"I'd like to help," I said, switching the phone to my other ear. We eventually got around to talking about how I might make a contribution. I admitted that I was recently out of college, living at home, and currently unemployed.

She laughed. "You already sound like you have all the credentials to become a Patron of Roethke. Being broke, but passionate, is a prerequisite." She paused a moment. "Seriously, though, I'd never turn away anyone who wants to help."

I promised her that I would get in touch when I came up with something.

The branch manager was still all over my résumé. He hummed little noises of disbelief or puzzled surprise. How many times could he read the damn thing from top to bottom? Leaning back, I crossed my arms. I slouched. Then, thinking of my old man, I sat up straight again. I was wearing one of his sports coats and one of his ties. I pushed a finger through a small hole in the coat near the elbow. I touched my skin and felt its cold.

The manager lowered my résumé again and looked me in the eye. He smiled, seeming pretty pleased with himself.

"BFA in Poetry," he said, scratching his forehead. "I'm guessing that doesn't mean the poetry of Business, Finance, and Accounting."

Something about his joke reminded me of my dad. "No," I said, shaking my head. "It's a Bachelors in Fine Arts."

Finger-brushing his comb-over into place, he looked at the paper again. "So it's a degree in English?" he asked, looking up at me.

I shook my head. "No, it's a degree in writing poetry."

He nodded slowly, fingers drumming the back of the paper. "Didn't know you could do that."

That was exactly what my dad had said when I called home to tell them I was changing my major. I had enrolled with the intention of becoming a high school English teacher. I had a teacher in tenth grade, Mrs. Kelly, who really influenced my early reading. She took me aside, recommended books, and talked with me when I finished them. She made me feel less alone, less of an oddball. I wanted to be that person for somebody else.

Then I got to college and took an Introduction to Creative Writing course with Professor Smith. He told us on the first day to call him Kurt. "I don't really profess," he told us, smiling, after somebody addressed him as Professor. I liked that. I'd never met anybody so passionate about poetry. After only five weeks in his class, I changed my major. The next fall, though, he was gone. He'd only been at the school on a one-year contract, filling in for somebody who was on sabbatical. I sometimes looked for him on the Internet, but the only thing I ever found was his poem "Little Sister Shining" which was published in an e-zine called *Poetry Matters*. The magazine had gone under, but its archives were still online. Other than that, he had virtually disappeared, which meant he probably didn't find another teaching position.

My mom had been excited about my new major. "You can't go wrong if you follow your passion," she said. At forty-three years old, she hadn't planned on being a mother. At fifty, my dad was probably even more surprised to be a father. They'd been told that they couldn't have children. Then, oops, I came along. I don't know if she'd always been a romantic—maybe it had something to do with the unlikelihood of my birth—but my mother supported me in almost anything I wanted to try.

Then, there was my dad.

"What happened to teaching?" he asked. "Poetry? What the hell kind of job you going to be able to get with a degree like that?"

In hindsight, it was a good question.

The manager set my résumé on his desk. He looked at me, scratched his cheek, and then slowly rubbed his palms together, like a housefly. "You took other classes, too, right? Accounting or Economics?"

I guessed that he didn't want to hear about the astronomy class I dropped because the math formulas involved for calculating the distances between celestial bodies were too difficult. I racked my brain for something he might want to hear. I shrugged. "I took a one-credit summer course in scansion."

He sat up, smiling. "Never heard of it. What is it?"

I made little chops with my hand through the air and told him how it involved dividing a poem up into feet. The face he made suggested that he was trying to figure out what mental disorder I might have. *Who is this idiot who thinks poems have feet?*

I pressed on, my hands sliding around in front of me like I was doing Tai Chi. "You look at the different stresses of each syllable." His face didn't change, and I started to feel pretty stupid. "It's really pretty technical," I said, crossing my arms.

He looked at me and pressed his fingertips together and up into a steeple. "Well, we don't really do that here."

I shrugged my hands into the air. "I took Logic, too." It counted toward the university's math requirement. *Math requires mathematical thinking. Logic is like math. Therefore, those who are good in Logic must be able to think mathematically…and therefore* work at a bank. I could tell by his furrowed brow that he wasn't arriving at the same syllogism.

He picked up my résumé again and then a second piece of paper. He looked back and forth between the two. This guy believed in paper. "You did really well on the assessment test that we emailed to you."

I shrugged. "Seemed like pretty common sense questions."

He looked at me seriously. "Even so, sixty percent of applicants don't pass it." He turned back to the papers again.

I smiled and reached over to my left hand and spun my ring around my finger, looking at the Fordite in the setting—halos of blue, red, orange, white and black. My parents gave it to me when I graduated from high school. My mother explained that the colorful stone wasn't a stone at all. "It's called Detroit Agate," my father said. "It was scraped from the walls of the spray paint booths in the Ford River Rouge car plant." He said that they took chunks of paint from the conveyors and then cut and polished them into gems. Kaleidoscope patterns emerged depending on the angle of the cut or the depth of the polishing. "They switched to different technology for painting cars, so Fordite is getting pretty rare," Dad said. When I told my mom how much I liked the ring, she made it clear that it was my father's idea.

The manager cleared his throat. "Do you have any other experiences or education that might relate to the position that you can think of?"

I blinked and then looked at him. "This is just a teller position, isn't it?" It was the wrong question.

He set the two pieces of paper on his desk and fussed with them until they lay perfectly parallel to each other. His face was solemn. "Tellers are our front line, the first faces our customers meet."

"I'm pretty sure I know how to count money back to people." I regretted saying it as soon as it came out. I tried to recover. "I worked at the university's writing center. I have pretty good people skills."

He leaned back in his chair and threaded his fingers behind his head. "Writing center? Writing center." I could tell that he didn't know what the hell a writing center was…and, he wasn't going to ask. He'd already made the mistake of asking about scansion, and look where that had gotten him. He exhaled. "What kind of future would you see for yourself at the bank?"

Future? What the hell was this guy talking about? Was I asking for the bank's hand in marriage? Was it his daughter? "I don't know." I shrugged. "I guess I'd be here for at least a year."

His smile was fatal, as was his diminutive nasal exhale. "Most of our applicants want to break into banking," he said, shrugging his palms. "They see a position like this as a stepping stone. Many of us in management started out as tellers ourselves."

I could feel the job, like loose sand, slipping through my fingers. Had it really ever even been in my hand? I adjusted myself in the seat and threw my palms up. "I mean, I really don't know. It could end up being something longer term. I'd have to see."

An email notification chimed from his computer. We both pretty much knew that I wasn't going to get the job. Still, he didn't even try to pretend with a sideways glance. Instead, he turned fully toward his monitor and started reading the email. He laughed quietly. After a few seconds, he actually started to type a response.

I made a noise in my throat.

He swiveled toward me and, I swear to God, he looked surprised to see me still sitting there. He smiled, but very unlike the way he'd smiled at the email. "Well, I think I have everything I need from you," he said. He stood up, thanked me for coming in, and handed my résumé back to me.

Yes, he actually gave my résumé back to me.

When I stood, he extended his hand. I felt the wet cold of my palm in the dry warmth of his.

"You should think about changing that to a BFA in English or maybe a BA in Communications." He smiled in a way that only included himself. "Or BS." He winked. "I'm just kidding."

I looked at him, my hand still frozen in his. That degree...it was four years of my life. It wasn't a joke.

"For a lot of people, that poetry stuff is going to be a head scratcher," he said. "It doesn't even sound like a real degree." He took his hand back. "English or Communications—at least people can wrap their minds around those, you know?"

"Yeah," I said, not really knowing what I was saying. Something simmered along my spine as I walked toward the door. Standing at the threshold, I turned back to him. He was nothing but a blur in my angry vision, sitting in the glow of his monitor.

"You can shove this job up your ass," I stammered. Reaching for the wall switch, I flipped it on, flooding the room in bright fluorescence.

"Hey!"

Running through the lobby, I knocked over a wastebasket of crumpled deposit slips and receipts. I righted it again and bolted for the door. One of the tellers called after me: "Have a good day."

Outside a cold rain was drizzling. I jogged along the strip mall's sidewalk and took cover near the doors of a clothing store. Nobody from the bank was following me. I didn't know why I expected it. Would he really have bothered to chase me? He probably shook his head, got up from his desk, and turned the light off again. Like that, he'd put me out of his mind. He had emails to answer. I was nothing to him. A blip. A momentary infraction of the bank's sustainability policy. An anecdote to laugh about with his wife that night.

I leaned against the cold brick wall and looked out over the flat, sprinkling gray of Saginaw. I glanced down at my résumé.

EDUCATION
· BFA in Poetry, University of Michigan

Every school Heather applied to had offered her a teaching assistantship. She called me to complain about how hard it was to decide what offer to accept. She'd asked me about my offers. I lied and told her that I was still waiting to hear.

My head hurt. I was thumping it against the brick wall behind me without really knowing it.

Fuck.

Balling my résumé up in my fist, I stared out from under the canopy. The drizzle turned into a steady rain. My dad had offered to drive me to the interview. I'd told him that I was fine with walking.

When it was clear that the rain wasn't going to let up, I stepped out into it and started the long trek home.

3.

Shivering and soaking wet, I stopped at the bottom of the basement stairs. A light near the furnace shined along the wall like a colossal firefly. It was my father—white hair glowing faintly—crouching along the foundation, following the halo of a flashlight. That had always been his way... always on hands and knees, or behind an appliance with the back off, or up on the roof re-caulking the flashing around the chimney. Guessing that he hadn't heard me come down, I turned in the other direction and started for the dim outline of a door on the far wall.

"Letting up out there?"

I turned. His back was still to me. "Getting worse," I said.

He shook his head. "Sonuvabitch." As he went down on both knees, I watched his finger in the spotlight. It slid along the mortar between two of the wall's cinder blocks. "This whole wall is compromised. We had all that runoff from the snow and then the rain—"

I crossed my arms. He was working up a real head of steam to tell me all about the problems with the basement. Again. "Dad, I'm dripping wet here. I just want to get out of these clothes."

He turned the beam of light on me. "Make sure you hang my sports coat above the dehumidifier," he said, after a second. "I only have the one that's any good."

Squinting, I held up a hand and shaded my eyes. "Yeah, I will." I walked away from the light.

Opening the door, I pulled the cord to the single bulb overhead. When I first got back home, I put the makeshift bedroom together for myself. My mom had once stored all of her jams and preserves here. I didn't know what my dad had done with her jars and lids, but the shelves were all still intact. I was using them for my books.

A friend of mine had helped me get a job with a big-box bookstore in Ann Arbor back at the end of April. For whatever reason, I had imagined myself working the register and helping people locate their favorite titles. Instead, they put me in the loading dock unloading skids of books. After five days, my back and arms ached

24

so much every morning that I could barely move. I hadn't gone to college for four years to do that kind of work. I didn't really quit officially. I just didn't come in for two days. On the afternoon of the second day, a voice on the answering machine told me that I was fired. I listened to the message play out and then turned over and went back to sleep.

I hung my father's coat and tie above the hum of the dehumidifier and then changed into sweats. Rubbing a towel over my head, I slid *Walden* from my shelf. I'd been thinking about it ever since the interview, trying to remember what Thoreau had written about the dehumanizing nature of paid labor. After some flipping around, I found it:

Most men, even in this comparatively free country, through mere ignorance and mistake, are so occupied with the factitious care and superfluously coarse labors of life that its finer fruits cannot be plucked by them. Their fingers, from excessive toil, are too clumsy and tremble too much for that. Actually, the laboring man—

My dad banged on the door, as though he could sense Thoreau bad-mouthing him.

"Yeah?"

He opened the door. Walking across the room, he crouched in one of the corners. "Just gotta check the walls in here."

"Knock yourself out," I said, flopping back on the bed.

After a moment, he made a frustrated noise.

"What is it?"

"You got water seeping through the mortar in here, too," he said.

I flipped a page. "That's a bummer."

His knees popped when he stood up. I looked over the top of the book. He wasn't leaving. He was just standing there, shaking his head at the wall. "Looks like I'll be able to plug this leak with hydraulic cement," he said. "I can see right where it's coming in."

Going back to the book, I made an affirming noise in my throat.

I heard him scratching the back of his neck. "See, the weeping tiles under the house were all plugged up with sand this spring, so when—"

I slapped the book shut. "So when the snow started to melt, you had a flood down here...You told me all this already. The bricks near the floor are all 'compromised,' and you've had water seeping in ever since."

I regretted the silence that followed. Right after saying them, I could always hear in the resonance the things I should have kept to myself. Too bad I had almost no ability to predict and censor them in advance.

He scratched his neck again and looked at me sideways. "You don't have to stay down here, you know. This damp can't be good for your books." He sniffed. "You could stay in the guestroom, for Christ's sake. It's still your room."

I lay the book on my chest. Just standing there staring at me, he looked really old under the harsh light of that single bulb. At his age, most men were grandfathers. "I'm fine down here, Dad." He looked frail, weak even. I picked up the book and opened it again. The words were a blur.

I watched him moving toward the shelves. He stood in front of them for a moment before speaking. "Your mother used to be in here all the time," he said, his voice misty. He reached out as though he half suspected he'd find a jar of zucchini preserves among my books. Instead, he slid out a volume of Anne Sexton's poetry, turned it over, and looked at the author photo on the back.

"Pretty lady," he said.

I lay in the knowledge of my mother being gone, Sexton being gone...everything good that becomes gone.

He slid the book back into its place and cleared his throat. "So, you a bank teller now?"

"I highly doubt it." It was becoming clear that going back upstairs wasn't a part of his immediate plans.

He flicked the flashlight on and then off again. "Didn't go well?"

"No, it went great. Turns out they want to make me the bank's president. Start Monday. Big salary, lots of responsibility."

He was quiet for a moment. I flipped a page, though I wasn't reading.

"It's a tough economy right now, Denver. I wouldn't—"

"That job wasn't worth losing sleep over."

"Well, still, you gotta find something. I mean, you want to, right? Something?" He waited a moment. "I know this guy—"

"Dad."

He pumped his palm at me. "Look, hear me out." He swallowed. "I got a friend, a supervisor of maintenance over at the River View Hotel—"

I puffed my cheeks and exhaled. "Jesus."

"Just listen, okay?" He took a step closer. "I pulled some strings and got you an interview on Monday. It's just a temp position. It's nothing you'd—"

"This is so typical." I closed the book and rested it on my chest again. "I don't know anything about working at a goddamn hotel."

"But you knew a lot about being a bank teller, right?" He shook his head. "You've been here over three weeks. Don't you think it's time you do something?" We stared at each other. He made the first move and took a few steps toward the door. Then he turned back and sighed. "I know it's not easy...figuring things out. At your age, I was trying to earn—"

"Dad."

He stopped and glanced up at me.

I held up the book. "I'm just going to read this, okay?"

"That's fine," he said, crossing his arms.

I opened the book and started to read. Sentences came into focus out of the blur. Silence was better than saying something I might regret.

After a moment, I could still feel him in the room, still looking at me.

"Don't get too involved in that, though," he said. "I want you to help me bring the patio furniture out of the garage."

"In the rain?"

He opened the door. "It'll probably let up, and, if not, then yeah...in the rain."

"What, you got people coming over for a barbecue tonight?"

"Don't be such a smartass, will ya? Just don't let the time get away from you. I could use some help around here." He walked out and closed the door behind him, but not before adding, "for once."

I sat numb in the silence that settled into the room after he left—the "for once" still resonating in my head. I tried to get back into Thoreau's words, tried to lose myself, but I couldn't. I closed the book and let it drop to the floor. It took me a minute to realize it, but I was shivering. My damp hair. The damp basement. The forty-minute walk in the cold rain. Despite the dry sweatshirt and pants, the chill was in my bones. Or maybe it was just my dad, like he'd brought the room down by fifteen degrees.

I turned down the bed covers and crawled in. Lying on my side, I looked at the corner that he'd been fussing over. A drip of water swelled along the mortar and, when it was finally too heavy, broke loose and slid down the wall, adding to a small, shiny puddle on the floor. The next drop started to swell.

27

"He never works hard enough." "He always seems to disappear whenever there's work to be done." "He thinks he's too good for work." My dad had been saying things like that about me to my mother ever since I was ten years old. Back then, he'd heard that the paper route in the neighborhood was going to become available. Without asking me, he told the paperboy that I was interested in taking over. He even arranged for me to shadow the kid after school so I could learn the ins and outs of the job. The paperboy was fifteen years old. For two days, I followed him around on my bike while he showed me the different places that people wanted their papers left. It took about fifty minutes a day and didn't seem too bad. Seventeen dollars a week and really good tips around Christmas, he said.

Then Friday came. Collection day. We had to go around and knock on people's doors or ring their doorbells and tell them how much money they owed. Quite a few people were behind by a month or two, and the paperboy had to explain that if they didn't pay that he'd have to hold their papers because that was the policy. Hearing that, most of them paid. "Then hold 'em," one guy said. "I don't read the damn things, anyway." He slammed the door.

The paperboy made light of it. "Collecting's not that big of a deal. It's only once a month," he said as we walked between houses. Still, it bothered me. I knew that I wouldn't be able to pull off the line about the policy and holding the papers. When I was younger, I was shy—too shy for knocking on doors and hinting to adults that they were being deadbeats.

I went home that evening and told my mother that I didn't want to do it. "I'll explain to your father," she said. Later that night, I couldn't hear what they were saying, but I remembered lying in my bed listening to them talk. My father raised his voice. My mother's voice was soft and reasoned. She won him over. Even so, that was the beginning of the rift between us. He took me fishing a month later. "You're sure you want to go, right?" he asked me while we sat in the front seat of his truck. I smiled, nodding, oblivious to what he was getting at.

"You're not going to be too shy to talk to the guy at the bait shop are you?" he asked. "I mean, he might try to say hello, and I wouldn't want you to panic."

Asshole.

When I turned sixteen, it only got worse. As far as he was concerned, I should have been working twenty-five to thirty hours a week after school and on weekends—"earning my dues"—and not reading books like a hermit up in my room. He'd worked during high school, so why shouldn't his son? My mom always came to my defense: "He's getting very good grades, Lee. That is his job right now."

Pulling the blankets tighter around me, I watched the water drip from the mortar and thought of my mother. If I closed my eyes, I could still see her perfectly.

A grinding sound from the first floor jarred me out of a half sleep. My father sliding the patio door closed. Ten years ago, a doctor had told him that he needed to quit smoking. Dad came up with his own plan. He would have exactly one cigarette a day. He'd heard somewhere that it was almost the same thing as being a non-smoker. So that's what he did. Every night, just before dinner, he'd go out on the patio and have his one cigarette. Just one, every night. That's discipline, man.

I wasn't sure how long I'd been in bed, but I wasn't cold anymore. I threw off the covers and slid *Walden* back on the shelf. A lined piece of paper lay on my desk where the week before I'd started a new poem:

> Blacktop workers are in danger
> from the velocity they preserve.
> Their bodies, sculpted by labor
> and the sun are still
> soft targets for charging steel.
> Like rivet work on skyscrapers,
> there is the threat of death
> every time they clock in.
> But there are no safety
> cables on the shoulders
> of an interstate, just
> trusting roadmen hoping America
> will kindly slow down
> from its fevered pursuit
> of happiness.

I shook my head. So much about the poem was bad…so heavy-handed. It was trying too hard to make an argument. That ending. Jesus. As had been pointed out to me in so many workshops, I wasn't trusting my images. "You're telling your reader what to think rather than letting the images make them feel." There were horrible lines like "soft targets for charging steel" and "there are no safety/ cables on the shoulders/ of an interstate." Seth Olson said it to me once in workshop: "There's never anything poetic about your poems. They just come out swinging, you know?

29

Sloppy left hook after sloppy left hook. Over and over." One of my professors called my work didactic. I had to look that one up in the dictionary, and it sure as hell didn't sound like a compliment. Overly moralizing.

I could see it, too. It was right there in front of me, exactly what they'd been talking about. Four years of school, and I was still doing it—sloppy left hooks intended to beat the reader into understanding. If I were in a workshop, they would have helped me. They would have salvaged something from the poem. They would have pointed out how I could use images to suggest what I was thinking. Give me advice, and I could revise. Give me three or four conferences with a professor, and I could write a decent poem.

On my own, I couldn't write shit. Or, that was the problem… all I could write was shit. Once piece after another.

Crumpling the paper in my fist, the noise like fire, I squeezed it until my fingers ached. I left it in a ball on the desk.

I lay back on the bed. The dehumidifier clicked into its droning. I stared up into the ceiling, trying to think myself out of what I'd been considering. For a minute, it didn't seem like I would do it. Then, I leaned over the edge of the mattress and picked the phone up out of its cradle. "Dumbass," I said, even as I punched in the number.

Her hello came out like a laugh. She'd been drinking, I could tell. Her intoxication might have been the only reason that she took my call.

"What's up, H?" I'd never called her H before. Maybe it was my subconscious way of telling her that my feelings toward her had become abbreviated.

Smooth. Really smooth.

"Denver? What are…how are you doing—Hold on." She laughed. "Are you going to tell her?" she whispered to someone on her end. "You'd make good connections." She laughed again.

Calling her…what a mistake. I cleared my throat. "Sounds like you're busy."

Somebody on her end burst out laughing. "We're at a bar," she said, laughing herself. "We had this marathon workshop with Elissa Gotti. She asked a couple of us out for drinks."

"She cool?" I was beyond verbs.

Heather laughed again, but it was a laugh that didn't really include me. "We don't know. We think she's hitting on Rachel. Elissa just went to the bar to get another drink, and Rachel's trying to get me to switch seats with her."

I didn't know Rachel. I'd only heard of Elissa because of Heather. Most likely, I didn't really know Heather anymore. "Well, I won't keep you," I said.

"No, wait, I'm going to go outside for a cigarette. I want to talk to you." She laughed. "Rachel's grabbing my arm trying to get me to stay," she explained.

I exhaled a laugh to say that I also found their situation funny, which I didn't. Her palm covered the mouthpiece. Then muffled talking. Laughter.

"Denver? I'll call you right back, okay?"

"Sounds good... just use the same number you used before. Do you still have it?"

She hung up.

I reached over, brought the phone's base up to my chest, and set the receiver back in the cradle. I could still hear her voice, her words: "I want to talk to you." Thinking back over our relationship, I remembered it being pretty good. It was when we started getting competitive and argumentative about our writing that things started to sour. Since she probably no longer felt in competition with me— Christ, she'd left me so far behind in that arena—maybe she was remembering Denver Hoptner, the person. Maybe her memories weren't so bad.

Early on, we were both night owls. Two, three, and sometimes four o'clock in the morning we'd just get up and go for long walks all over Ann Arbor. The streets were different without any cars. You could almost feel everyone sleeping, the whole town quietly breathing. We'd talk. One time she'd told me about how her father split when she was really young. "Mom worked two different jobs to keep us in our house. A few years later, she eventually remarried Kevin. Before that, though, Mom was always so tired." Heather told me that she'd make her mom tomato sandwiches. "Every night I'd make her one when she'd get home from waitressing. Simple stuff...just bread, tomato slices, olive oil, and salt. She loved them. Even when I was only eleven years old, I could feel that there was something about it, something good. Without being asked, I made those sandwiches almost every night. It was like I was a little nun, part of the Holy Order of Tomato Sandwiches or something."

I'd told her that she needed to write a tomato sandwich poem. She laughed. It was after that conversation that I knew I loved her. We kissed for awhile just within the threshold of an alley. Tongues and teeth, the warmth of her lower back against my palm.

31

I was nearly asleep again when the phone rattled my chest. I let it ring two more times before picking up. Couldn't be too anxious. Everything with Heather lately had to be games.

"Sorry," she said, "Elissa came back with White Russians for us. She didn't let us touch them until the ice started to melt, and then—"

"Hello?"

Oh, Christ. "I got it, Dad...it's for me."

"Oh, okay." He took a breath. "Don't be too long. I made Spam and eggs."

That sounded really impressive. Heather was at a bar outside of Fallingbrook drinking White Russians with Elissa Gotti, and I was in Shit Stain, Michigan eating Spam and eggs with my old man. That had to be making her feel the sting of our breakup. How did she ever let me get away?

"Dad, hang up."

He did.

"So you're outside, now?" I asked, listening to her suck in a drag.

"Yeah...what a gorgeous evening." She laughed. "Spam, huh? You have to love the way it slides out of the can."

I made a noise in my throat, hoping she would say something about how she wished I was there with her. She didn't. "We got rain here," I said. She took another drag. I imagined her pursed lips and the way she tilts her neck and exhales toward the sky. She had such a pretty neck. What did I have?

Spam and rain.

"So," she started, "I got some really unbelievable news today."

Writing news. Something cold raced into my fingers. "Oh, yeah?"

She purred an affirmative note. "Remember how I was a runner-up for that Ragdale fellowship?" She paused just long enough for me to realize what she was about to tell me. "Well, the woman who got it can't go. They called me today, and I'm going."

Good writing news like that for someone else always made me think about my own lack of success. Back in school, Andy Tanner came into workshop one night and announced that he'd sent a poem to the *Nebraska Review*, and they'd accepted it. Everyone was instantly reflective, and then sullen. Even Professor Smith seemed a little deflated. "Well, hey," he offered after a moment, "That's big news." The way he said it, though, it was like he was saying, "Well, hey, that's certainly a lot bigger than anything I've had happen." It was ironic too because when Andy had brought the poem in for workshop six weeks earlier, we'd all really ripped it apart. He made a point of telling us that the version the *Nebraska Review* had accepted was the same version he'd brought to workshop that night. He looked at Professor Smith. "You said that in the end we have to learn to trust our own voices, so that's what I did," he said, beaming. "That's true," Professor Smith said, nodding weakly. "Good for you."

I flipped the pillow over to the cool side. "Ragdale? That's Chicago, right?"

"Lake Forest...really close to Chicago."

I wrapped the phone cord around my finger, watching the tip turn purple. "That's really great. Congratulations."

"I still can't believe it," she said. "I leave Fallingbrook, visit my folks for two weeks, and then head straight to Ragdale. Arthur Mervin is going to be there to give a reading while I'm there. They say he really doesn't do many appearances."

I switched the phone to my other ear. "You know, whenever I see his name, it always makes me think of Merlin."

"What?"

"Nothing." I sat up with my back against the wall. God, was I moron. Fucking Merlin? "You're doing really big things. I'm proud of you, H."

"Thanks...D." She probably meant it playfully, but when she abbreviated my name, it sounded like she was giving me—my life—a grade.

She exhaled. "You know, Elissa said she's never even been to Ragdale."

The cinderblocks were cold against my back. Another thought came to me. "Are you driving to Chicago?"

She said that she would be.

"Really? Well, you should plan a little detour. Shoot up to Saginaw and spend a night at my dad's place...in the guestroom. I could show you the sites of the infamous Sag-nasty."

She paused. "Maybe. I'd have to check..." She took a long drag. "Wait a minute. I didn't even ask you. How did your interview go today?"

In so many words, she was telling me that there was no way in hell that she was coming to Saginaw. Spam, rain, and loser probably didn't really fit into her itinerary. "It was fine," I said, switching the phone again. "I got it, but then I turned them down. Can you see me working at a fucking bank? Next thing you know I'd be driving an SUV and investing in mutual funds."

She laughed. "Denver Hoptner, rebel poet."

"You know it."

Her lighter flicked. "So," she said, "are you working on anything? Any good poems in the works?"

Anymore, that was her go-to question. I sighed, looking at the balled up poem on my desk. I closed my eyes and rubbed the bridge of my nose. "I told you the other night that I'm not."

"Holy cow, if I had the time you have right now…I really need to look over my work. Elissa said I should be thinking about putting a manuscript together."

"Maybe she just likes your ass." In a different tone, it would have sounded like a joke. In my mouth, it sounded bitter. I tried to recover. "I mean, it's a nice ass. Who wouldn't like it, right?"

She didn't say anything for a moment. "Denver, you should really think about doing a retreat. They can be really good for your writing."

"Retreats cost money." I shifted the pillow up between my back and the wall. "I don't think I really buy into that, anyway."

"What do you mean?"

"All of it, I guess…the whole poetry scene. Retreats and networking and writing programs. It's all so much bullshit." I squeezed my hand into a fist and then released it. "Poets writing for other poets is all it ends up being. I mean, you sit around pretending that you have an audience, but what you're doing doesn't really matt—"

"You seemed to buy into it enough when you were applying to grad schools."

It was like she'd reached through the phone and slapped me. I could feel the subtext of what she was saying: "You know, the grad schools that you couldn't get into?"

I swallowed. "I know, I know, but it's easy to get caught up in, you know? Grad schools and publication…it's easy to think that all of that shit means something. When you're in school or in workshop, you actually start to believe—"

She sniffed in an interrupting breath. "Sounds like sour grapes to me."

A silence settled between us. I hadn't wanted things to go this way. The phone rested like a clothes iron against my hot ear. "You know, I was just—"

Laughter rippled in the background on her end of the call. Voices called to her, and her palm scraped over the receiver. Her muffled voice rose in pitch to meet theirs, until I couldn't distinguish who was speaking.

For her, I was gone.

She came back. "Look, Denver, I have to get going." She paused. "You should really think about talking to someone. You sound a little depressed."

"I'm not depressed." I touched my thumb against a finger and fought the urge to tell her to kiss my ass. "Look, don't call me anymore, okay," I said, unable to get my voice much above a whisper. "Find someone else to brag to."

She was laughing at something when she hung up. I wasn't sure if she had heard what I said. I hoped she did.

Then, a few seconds later, I hoped she hadn't.

4.

Yawning, I walked up out of the basement and into the kitchen. On the radio in the living room, two sports commentators were trading remarks about a Tigers game. The murmur of the crowd hummed under their talking. The sound of it brought me back to being a little kid. Most summer weekends I was in the garage with my dad handing him tools or watching him at the workbench. Back then, he didn't really seem to mind that I was shy and that I didn't hang out with the neighborhood kids. I think he even liked having me around. It wasn't until middle school that I started to choose spending time in my room with comic books over time in the garage with him and baseball. "Nothing like a ballgame on the radio," my dad would say. Up until the end of fifth grade, I agreed with him.

"Who's winning?" I shouted toward the living room.

He called back to tell me that they were playing the Indians.

"So, you're telling me that the Tigers are losing."

"You got it."

"Another one, two, three inning for the Tribe," one of the commentators said. "The Tigs gotta get those bats going."

"Dinner's on the stove," Dad shouted. "Hope you like your eggs cold."

Lumpy, dried out scrambled eggs and three fogged-over pieces of Spam sat in the frying pan. I dumped all of it onto a plate, covered it in plastic wrap, and set it in the microwave. I had fallen asleep again after getting off the phone with Heather. Squeezing a hand over my forehead, I recalled what I'd said to her before hanging up. Not good.

When the microwave beeped, I looked at the time. Six thirty. I needed to get going to Old Town before too long. It was the second time I was hosting an open mic at the coffee shop. The first night there were people, but not the crowd I'd hoped for. Since that time, I'd done more promoting. I'd pinned up fliers on the bulletin boards at the university and community college. The Saginaw paper even ran the press release I'd sent in: The Rage for Roethke Open mic Reading. I made it clear that it was a fundraiser, and that I'd be taking—

36

Something outside caught my eye, something different. I suddenly realized what I was seeing.

Patio furniture.

A chill ran through me—a shudder of guilt. He had dragged all of the furniture out of the back shed and up onto the patio while I napped. The table, its heavy glass top, the chairs. The bulky Adirondacks. I leaned to see it, and there it was...the wrought-iron bench that no man my father's age should have been moving by himself. I imagined, too, that the whole time he was grunting and straining himself close to a hernia that he was picturing me in my bed with my nose in that book. He could have called for me. I would have come.

Exhaling, I took my plate into the living room and sat on the couch by the front window. He was in his recliner next to the radio, sipping a beer. He didn't look at me.

Sawing it off, I chewed a piece of the salty meat. "Good eats," I said.

He looked at me and smiled. "Even better hot out of the pan," he said, taking another drink.

I swallowed. "Sorry. I fell asleep."

"It happens."

What he probably meant was that it happens all the time with a son like me. I chewed up a forkful of eggs. "You know, you should have waited. I would have helped you with the furniture."

"Don't worry about it. Little exercise is good for me." He held his beer can up to his face and turned it in his fingers like he was trying to read the ingredients. "So, who called?"

"Hmm? Oh, nobody...just somebody I knew from school." I couldn't imagine where she might be. Whatever world she was living in, it was beyond my imagination. She was out there somewhere with White Russians and Rachel and Elissa Gotti, the cutting-edge, lesbian poet. She wasn't giving me a second thought. "It was just an old girlfriend," I said.

Dad circled his finger around the rim of the can and then took a sip. "Still something there?"

I finished another bite of eggs. "For me a little. Not for her."

He smiled sympathetically. "Sorry," he said, scratching his head. "What's she doing calling you?"

I pierced another piece of Spam and shrugged. "I don't know. I guess she still wants to be friends. She likes to keep me up to date on what's going on in her life."

Dad shook his head. "Jesus, why do they do that?"

I chewed the Spam. "I do not know."

We listened to the game while I finished eating. The Tigers seemed close to a rally, but the next two batters left runners stranded on second and third. Then, start of the next inning, a batter for the Indians, Grady Sizemore, swung at the first pitch he got and smacked it toward left field.

"That ball is gone," one of the announcers said.

"They never fail to disappoint." Dad reached over and turned off the radio. He took a drink of his beer and then rested the can on his knee.

I sat with the empty plate on my lap.

He cleared his throat. "All of Mom's books are still in the backroom, you know. You could go through them and take whatever ones you want."

I nodded and told him that I would. Mom's recliner sat next to him on the other side of the little table. Nobody ever sat in it anymore. I could still picture how she looked sitting in it, reading a book.

Like he was imagining the same thing, Dad shook his head and looked at her seat. "She sure loved to read."

I took a deep breath and stood up to check the time.

"Grab me another beer if you're going into the kitchen."

"You got it."

After setting the plate in the sink, I went back down to my room and changed into jeans and a black shirt. I checked my hair in the mirror. It looked okay, even having slept on it. The puddle on the floor had grown a little bigger.

I came back into the living room and handed Dad his beer.

"Thanks," he said, cracking it open and giving my clothes a onceover. "So, what do you think," he asked, "you going to go to that interview?"

I stood by the front window and looked out at the road. I took a long breath and exhaled it slowly. "I don't know...I doubt it."

"Well, give it some thought. The guy's an old friend. I'm going to look pretty stupid calling him back to tell him that you're not—"

"Shit, Dad, I don't want to work at some goddamn hotel." I crossed my arms and kept my back to him. I bit my lower lip and then released it. "Nobody asked you to set this up for me."

"I know," he said after a moment. "I was just trying to help." A few seconds later, he turned the radio on again. It was a commercial. He turned the volume down.

I sat on the couch studying my hands and spinning that Fordite ring around my finger.

Dad sighed. "Look, I'll call him back, then." He said that it was no skin off his teeth. "You'll find something, right?"

I glanced up, and he smiled.

"There's more beer in the fridge," he said. "Grab yourself one, and we can sit here and listen to the rest of this heart-breaking game."

I shrugged. "I can't. I'm going out."

Buckling his lips in against his teeth, he nodded his head slowly for a few seconds. "Of course you are." The game came back on, and he turned up the sound.

"It's just that I have to—"

He held up his hand. "Save it. I don't even want to know."

"No, come on, Dad. I would stay...I would. It's just that I have that open mic that I've been—"

"I told you...I'm not interested."

I crossed my arms and slouched back into the couch. "Fine."

A second Tiger in a row struck out. I stood up and looked out the window.

Dad's voice came into the room behind me like a haunting. "You know, Denver, when you called me from Ann Arbor to tell me that you wanted to move back home, you said you wanted to spend some time with me...look after me."

I turned around and looked at him. "What?"

He toasted his beer can toward me. "You're doing one goddamn of a bang-up job, son."

Something chilling washed through me. I tried to remember if that was really what I'd said. "Dad, I—"

He nodded. "Seriously. Leaving me alone every chance you get...there's no doubt about it, you're one helluva comfort." He toasted his beer higher and then finished it off in one long gulp.

"Dad."

He stood up. "This might be news to you," he said, "but the insurance didn't cover everything with Mom's treatment...not by a long shot."

I smoothed the fingertips of my left hand slowly down one cheek. Mom's cancer had been so sudden, so aggressive. I remembered talking to her on the phone or visiting her. She never talked about her treatment. Dad, on the other hand, that's all he talked about. He recognized a kindred spirit in the oncologist, a man who wanted to fix things, no matter the odds. Like Dad, he had all kinds of tools and was ready to use them. They tried everything, even shark cartilage capsules along with standard therapies. All of that was during my junior year at U of M. The funeral was in July before my last semester. When I got back to Ann Arbor in August, my friendship with Heather moved into the bedroom. While Mom was sick, I took a bus home every other weekend to see her. After she died, I didn't come home at all, not even for Thanksgiving. Even this past Christmas, I told Dad's answering machine that I was going to spend the holiday working in a soup kitchen. My strategy for trying to forget about Heather.

It didn't work.

"Look, Dad, I would stay tonight. I even want to, but I have that fund—"

"I don't even care about that." He waved his hand at me. "I've listened to plenty of ball games by myself. What I need you to do is start pulling your weight around here…maybe even pay a little rent." He crossed his arms. "I'm trying to dig out of a hole here." Not looking my way, he walked out of the room.

I turned to the window again, taking in a deep breath and exhaling it slowly. I heard him open the patio door and slide it shut behind him. Looking through the kitchen, I could see his silhouette sitting at the patio table, the other empty chairs dark shadows around him. The orange cherry of a cigarette hovered in front of him. He brought it up to his mouth. As far as I knew, this was the first time he'd ever had two in one day since making his pact. I turned back to the window.

I was shaking.

"That's the third error in this inning alone," one of the commentators said. "It's like their heads aren't in this game at all."

5.

Nobody was really listening to the poem. It was just as well. With his long, blonde hair pulled back into a ponytail and wearing all black, the guy at the microphone scrawled only a one-word moniker—Coyote—on the sign-up sheet when he came in. Ignoring the others who were reading, he sat by himself at a table scribbling on a napkin and sometimes laughing at or nodding about what he was writing. He sat on his chair with it turned backwards toward the table. When it was his turn to read, he brought the napkin to the mic, unfurled it, and explained to the audience that he subscribed to the spontaneous bop prosody approach to writing verse. "I literally wrote this in five minutes," he said. Then, he started reading.

Listening to the poem, my guess was that he didn't even use the entire five minutes.

Somewhere in the middle of the poem, he held the napkin at arm's length and then brought it in close to his face. "I can't even read th…wait a minute, I got it:

America's star falls into chaos
the donkeys and elephants
can't fix this Zen-less mess"

He pronounced the last word as "may-oss," a sudden, unprecedented moment of southern drawl.

Most of the people crowded around the small tables were there to get a cup of coffee, not an earful of bad poetry. A few of them, who had no choice but to sit close to the open mic area, gave obligatory applause when Coyote finished. They patted their hands together exactly three times, never even glancing away from their conversations. They might as well have been swatting flies. I couldn't really blame them. Every poem tonight had ranged from horrible to almost amateur.

The handful of people who were actually there for the poetry were a little more gracious. Two overweight high school girls who'd been to the first open mic slapped their hands together vigorously. A third snapped her fingers and then smiled knowingly at her friends

41

as though fulfilling a dare, the promise I imagined her making on the way over in the car: "I'm going to snap my fingers whenever someone finishes reading a poem, you guys!"

"No way!"

"Way!"

A couch of guys in black shirts and skinny jeans applauded, though they seemed unimpressed. I overheard them talking about an Introduction to Creative Writing class that they were taking at the local university. They were starting their poetry initiation and had, apparently, some idea of what to be unimpressed by. Nothing was going to impress them, except their own poems, which would, of course, be viewed as brilliant.

To thank the audience for their tepid response, Coyote howled. I'm not kidding, he fucking howled.

Unreal.

Sitting with an acoustic guitar between his legs, Joshua Palmer—not Josh—smiled and hooted a "woo" in reply.

The whole place was becoming a wildlife preserve before my eyes.

Tonight was Joshua's second appearance. I had hoped that the open mic would stay strictly poetry. Of course, I couldn't have very easily turned Joshua away when he showed up that first night, guitar case in hand, and put his name on the sign-up sheet. He had sung "The Wreck of the Edmund Fitzgerald" which, admittedly, had been a crowd favorite. He was a good singer, I gave him that much.

Sitting off to the side wearing wire rim glasses and with his hair in cornrows, Heywood Peoples managed to look scholarly and street at the same time. He emitted no animal noises. His laced fingers rested in his lap stoically.

He'd shown up to the first open mic but hadn't read. He just listened. Afterwards, he and I talked for over an hour, and he showed me some of his poetry. It was raw, but really good. I had asked him where he'd taken classes. He hadn't. When I asked him why he didn't sign up to read, he said he didn't feel ready. I worked on him and told him that he had to come back the next week and read something. Looking at the floor, he said that he would.

I was really glad to see that he'd shown up.

I waited, but Coyote didn't leave the microphone. He rubbed his hands together. "I know I'm only supposed to read one poem but, man, I wrote this earlier," he said, "and I gotta go with it. I'm just feeling it, you know?" He pulled a paper bag from his back pocket—the long, skinny kind used for bagging bottles of wine. He unfolded it and started to read from it:

> Highways, long and black
> I think of Kerouac,
> Jack, still out there
> Somewhere
> A burning Buddha angel gypsy…

Bruce Taylor pulled on my sleeve. Hair parted down the middle and wearing a white polo and khakis—his signature look—he seemed like he would be more comfortable as the assistant manager of a Radio Shack rather than owning Old Town Saginaw's most popular coffee shop.

"I thought you had a rule about only one poem per reader."

I shrugged. "If I had a long hook, I'd pull him." Bruce's breath smelled of coffee and mouthwash.

"What's the point of rules if you're not going to enforce them?"

"You want me to tackle him?"

He leaned his hot, minty breath close to my ear. "Announce tonight's special again, okay…the way I told you?"

I inhaled heavily, but nodded.

"You remember it?"

"Yes."

He motioned toward Coyote. "He didn't buy anything, you know."

"Must have slipped under the radar."

Bruce held eye contact with me. "I told you that I don't want anyone signing up to read unless they're holding a drink…that they bought here," he said, pointing to one of the high school girls sucking on a milkshake from Burger King.

I shrugged my hands. "Like I said before, that's tough to enforce."

He told me that it wasn't difficult to enforce at all. "Just sit at the table where the sign-up sheet is," he explained, "and check for drinks before people sign up. You've got people taking up valuable table spa—"

"Looks like he's finished," I interrupted. "I better get up there."

"Don't forget the special," he called to my back.

Coyote got in one more howl before I was able to take the mic.

I thanked everybody for coming out. At a table full of college-age girls, a pretty blonde was watching me. I looked back at her. "If you're not here for the poetry, we still hope you're enjoying it." I smiled.

She turned her attention back to her friends.

"Free Bird!" a voice bellowed from the back. A few people laughed.

Joshua craned his neck, looking for the source of the request. He held his guitar up. "That could happen," he shouted, smiling.

Coyote looked up from his frenzied writing and howled again, which was followed by more laughter.

I waited a moment. Bruce was straining to make eye contact, so I nodded to him. "Before we get started, Bruce wanted me to let you know that he remains...cappuccino crazy. All cappuccinos and espressos are still ten percent off."

Cappuccino crazy. I actually had to say it.

Bruce threw his hands up. "What can I say? I'm a giver...I like to give," he shouted.

Laughter.

Before I could begin to introduce Heywood, the door opened. An older woman, probably in her late seventies, shuffled into the room. She had a composition book under one arm and a large, heavily decorated scrapbook in the other. One of the high school girls held the sign-up sheet and waved it. "I'll put your name down, Helen!"

Helen smiled and bobbed her head, making her way through the chairs.

"Helen...your usual tea?" Bruce asked, moving toward the counter.

"Yes, please," she said, taking her seat.

Bruce gave me a look that said, "Was that so hard?"

I tried to fight the disappointment I felt at Helen's arrival. I started the open mic because I wanted to bring poetry out of the university classroom and into the world. "At the very least, that's what the Beats had done," one of my lit professors had said. That's what d.a. levy had done—brought poetry back to street level. Still, would levy have tolerated Helen's poetry?

I knew Helen's story. She told it in detail at the first open mic, just before reading her poem. Her husband had died two years before, and the two of them had survived two adult children. She was alone. Scrapbooking and poetry were the two things that kept her going, she said. I guessed that her dog kept her going, too. Her poem was about him and included this little gem of a couplet:

Arthur, my naughty Pekingese,
to my dismay is leaking fleas.

44

When she finished reading all twelve stanzas, the crowd gave her a standing ovation. I was relieved that Heywood wouldn't have to follow her. Nobody could follow her.

Every open mic I'd ever attended had a Helen, if not a table full of them. They were the Ying to Coyote's Yang. Where Coyote made poetry seem like an accessory for under-informed, anti-establishment hipster douchebags, Helens made poetry seem quaint and harmless—a fitting hobby for widows and old retirees.

I don't think a single open mic has ever won poetry a new fan.

Helen settled in. I pointed to a bucket on the table in front of me. I reminded everyone why I was collecting donations. Bruce stared at me, probably wondering why I was directing money anywhere other than to his cash register. "They're having some financial trouble over at the Roethke House after a recent fire," I said. "You can help them out by pitching in anything you can give."

The bucket had a thin layer of coins across the bottom and maybe three or four dollar bills. "They're really strapped over there. So, seriously, let's help them put a roof back on Roethke's boyhood home," I said, clapping my hands.

A few people joined my clapping.

Coyote got up and ceremoniously set a napkin in the bucket. He smiled charitably. "A poem for the cause," he said.

The high school girl snapped.

I cleared my throat while Coyote remounted his chair. "Well, I've been looking forward to hearing our next poet's work," I said. The blonde turned around again and looked right at me. I smiled. "He tells me that this will be the first time he's read his poetry out loud, so I think we're all in for a real literary treat."

The blonde turned back to her group. I could read her lips well enough to see that she was mimicking the words "literary treat."

Her friends laughed.

Ignoring her, I looked at Heywood and smiled. His chest swelled with a deep breath that he exhaled slowly. "Everyone," I said, "please help me welcome Heywood Peoples."

I didn't expect much from the outlying crowd. Their applause was always involuntary, like a momentary tick. This time, though, even the other poets were reserved. The high school girl didn't even snap once. No yelp from Coyote. Maybe they were all put off by the special introduction I'd given Heywood.

His transition from sitting to standing was syrupy and cool. He drifted up to the podium and leaned into the mic as though it were a girl he was kissing for the first time.

His hands were empty. Whatever he was going to deliver to us, he had it memorized. That was smooth. I liked that.

"Red Streets," he said.

It was one of the poems he let me read the week before. I could still remember the ending:

> I can't really see,
> but I know
> what I can't see,
> your spilled heart, red
> in the pores of this cement
> that nothing, not even
> a thousand rains
> can wash away,
> not completely,
> little brother,
> not completely.

It was about his brother getting shot in a drive-by. He'd been mistaken for somebody else. Worried about him not arriving home on time, his mother took a walk to look for him. She'd found a group of people gathered around his body on the sidewalk. The poem was about how Heywood goes back to the spot all the time to talk with his brother, to remember him.

He let the title of the poem resonate for a moment. The room quieted:

> These red streets are hushed
> tonight, not rushed tonight.

His voice was unaffected and honest. No unnecessary inflection or melodrama.

> I'm on the sidewalk
> where my brother died,
> where my mother cried.

That got them. They were listening, leaning in...even some of the outliers. Even the blonde. There was hope for her, yet. Heywood kept reading:

> In this rare city silence—

46

The espresso machine grinded deafeningly. Heywood's eyes snapped toward Bruce behind the counter. A moment later, the sound died off. Bruce looked over his shoulder and said something laughingly to the waiting customer. He didn't notice Heywood's stunned posture, his glare. I clenched my fists.

Heywood recovered:

In this rare city silence—

The machine sounded again, like spoons getting run through a blender. Someone laughed. Then others.

Heywood looked at me. I shrugged and then nodded that he should keep going. He looked at Bruce. Then, after a moment, he smiled, shook his head, and drifted away from the podium like smoke and straight out the door.

"Bruce!"

He turned to look at me with the basket of grounds in one hand and a tamper in the other.

The place was silent. Finally.

I waved my arm toward the empty podium. "Seriously, man? You had to do that in the middle of a goddamn poem?"

Moving before I'd really even finished talking, I shoved open the door and stepped outside.

It was a warm night. Moist. The fishy smell of the Saginaw River permeated the air. Heywood leaned against a burned-out lamp post. He flicked a flame up to a Black and Mild.

"Hey, man," I said, walking over to him, "I'm really sorry about that."

He shrugged, blowing smoke out the side of his mouth. "No big thing…just a poem."

"Man, but it was your—"

The door to the coffee shop burst open behind me. Bruce was marching towards us and pointing an angry finger. "You know, Denver, I really don't appreciate that!" His neck was flushed red up to his ears. "Where do you get off talking to me like that in my place?"

He was inches from me. All I could see was that reddened neck and his lit-up eyes. As a kid, I was not only shy, but I was pretty timid, too. I hated anything physical. I backed down from fights in middle school, even ran from one. My dad did the whole "I'll teach you how to box" thing in the basement. It didn't take. I just wasn't a fighter.

I took a step back. My heart was really going, almost painfully. "Look, I'm sorry. I didn't—"

47

He pointed his finger in my face. "That was really out of line."

"I know, man...I know. I'm sorry. It's just that—"

He took another step into my space. "I want an apology. Now."

Heywood peeled himself from the lamp post and stood at my side. "Fuck that, man. He just did apologize. Twice."

Heywood was maybe five foot seven and probably under one hundred and twenty pounds, but he carried himself much bigger.

Bruce glared at him for a second.

"I ain't the one," Heywood said, smiling.

Bruce's eyes calculated the odds. He took a step back.

"You're right, Bruce," I said, "I shouldn't have blown up like I did. I know. It's just that...I mean, you gotta honor what's going on when someone is trying—"

He threw up his hands. The blood was fading out of his neck. "This isn't working out. This whole Poetry Thursdays...it's a bust."

With him out of my space, I felt a little of my fight come back, at least my verbal fight. I had been playing with the idea of calling Heather again and telling her that she could be a featured reader at the open mic. She might just swing up to Saginaw if her trip was connected to a reading. "Oh, come on, man. There are people in there... more than last week even. It'll grow every week if we give it a—"

"They aren't buying coffee." He pointed through the window. "That guy, that Coyote guy? He brought his own thermos with him, for Christ's sake."

A sound came from inside. Joshua was up at the mic strumming some opening chords. The crowd started clapping.

I crossed my arms. "It just needs more time. Word just needs to get—"

He shook his head. "It's just not working." He glanced at Heywood and lifted his chin. "Sorry about your poem," he said. "I didn't know." He turned and started to walk away.

"Bruce—"

With his retreating back to me, he held up a hand that silenced me. "It's done."

He opened the door and the chords and vocals poured out. The crowd clapped along as Joshua sang about changing his carnivorous habit, drinking carrot juice, and soaking up rays. The blonde was staring at him intently. Whatever smile she'd had for me...well, this one was bigger.

The door closed behind Bruce. Even so, it was easy to hear everyone erupt and sing the chorus right along with Joshua.

I shook my head and looked at Heywood. "'Cheeseburger in Paradise'? That's what people want to hear?"

Heywood dropped his cigarillo and stepped on it. "White folks, man...not too particular, not too precise."

I ran my fingers through my hair and crossed my arms again. "Jimmy Buffet can kiss my ass," I said.

"Amen to that, brother."

6.

Heywood was on the phone with his girl, talking in a soothing whisper. Outside were the headlights and taillights, the streetlights and the fluorescent lights of stores—all that light trying to reverse the darkness. We stopped at a red light. The dashboard glowed over us.

"I'll catch up with you later, boo," Heywood said.

She probably didn't understand why he was cruising around with some white boy from the township he'd met only a week earlier. I didn't exactly understand it myself.

After everything that happened at the coffee shop, Heywood had said, "Let's take a ride," and I'd said okay.

"Ah, baby, don't do that to me," he said into the phone, grinning.

She was probably telling him what he was missing, what he wasn't going to get even if he did show up later.

A pizza, ribs, and chicken place was lit up like a jack-o-lantern outside my window. It was some of the brightest light in the city, but jaundiced and sickly looking. We were on Michigan Avenue coming up on the Interstate.

Heywood whispered something before hanging up. A hole near his exhaust manifold coughed a little louder as he accelerated up the onramp toward I-675. Cracking his window, he touched the flame of his lighter to the stub of another cigar. The tall lights of the Henry Marsh Bridge's expanse over the Saginaw River glowed ahead of us.

Heywood hit the cigar like sucking on a straw.

A dim sky of constellations—the peppered lights of Saginaw's downtown—shined on the other side of the river. Black rectangles of buildings behind the lights almost looked like a living city in the darkness. The poverty was hidden. The drugs. The crime. The abandoned buildings. The skeleton fire and police departments.

The hopelessness.

I smelled something earthy and pungent. Heywood reached over and handed me what turned out to be the remaining quarter of a blunt.

I looked at the orange ember and then at him.

50

"You go to the kingdom, DH?"

I nodded. It'd been nearly two months. The last time I got high was after I'd heard from the last remaining grad school. Another acceptance without an assistantship. My roommate said there was only one thing to do under such circumstances. Afterwards, we ate two frozen pizzas and a bag of Funyuns…and we were still hungry.

I took a hit from the blunt and instantly felt my brain float up and rest against the inside of my skull. It was good bud. I passed it back.

Heywood took it into his fingers and thumb. He looked past me, out my window. "What the fuck is Beans, anyway?" he asked, taking another hit.

The word BEANS hovered neon green in the sky above the darkness of a defunct grain elevator. Behind the letters, in mid-leap, a neon pink jackrabbit flicked on and off.

It made me think of d.a. levy. Burned out by all the politics and the hostility between him and the Cleveland authorities, he played with the idea of publishing one issue of his magazine, *The Buddhist 3rd Class Junkmail Oracle*, full of sketches of rabbits. Just rabbits. No meeting anger with anger. No rants. No provocations. Just as he called it "a fuckin happy dump of rabbit sunlight" on the people here of Cleveland.

I imagined rabbits over Cleveland. A happy dump of rabbits. I giggled.

Heywood laughed. "Good shit, ain't it?"

I nodded, thinking of what my father had told me and then telling Heywood. It was one of my dad's favorite stories. The grain elevator under the jackrabbit used to be the headquarters of the Michigan Bean Company. Back in the 1920s, Harry Houdini came to Saginaw to do a show at the Jeffers-Strand Theater. "He was older and doing traditional magic tricks again," Dad said. He called a girl up from the audience to assist him with pulling a rabbit from a top hat. Afterwards, he let her keep the rabbit. "The girl was the daughter of the guy who founded the Michigan Bean Company." When they were trying to come up with a logo for the company years later, the old man told the story of his daughter and Houdini. He suggested a jackrabbit, and they went for it.

My father had always been into local history. When my mother was in her chair reading novels, my dad sat and read books like Truman Fox's *History of the Saginaw Valley*. Riding around town with him always meant getting a lesson. As a kid, I had liked listening to him.

51

Heywood passed the blunt again, and I hit it gingerly. My cheeks ached with smiling.

"Houdini?" Heywood said, shaking his head and laughing. "Fucking Houdini." He laughed. "Who Dini? You Dini." We had exited into the downtown. He was waiting to turn onto Washington. The semi-pro hockey arena was on our right. It filled up pretty well for most games, but afterwards people practically ran to their cars to get the hell out of the downtown.

I pointed to an empty lot. "There used to be a McDonalds there," I said.

Heywood nodded. "I know. They'll put a McDonalds anywhere. How fucked up your town got to be for them to take a McDonalds down?"

The Temple Theater's marquee flashed with red lights above us—a faint pulse on the nearly flat-lined stretch of the city's main drag. The opening of The Temple had put the Jeffers-Strand out of business. Now The Temple itself was struggling.

There were little poltergeists of activity around us. A man leaned down the sidewalk behind a shopping cart full of what looked like blankets. A few others slouched against the outside of the Bancroft, an old, ritzy hotel that the city had converted into low-cost housing. They were all shadows. Half-men loitering in a half-city.

I looked at Heywood. "Sorry about what happened with your poem."

"It's all good, man." He took the turn onto Genesee and started us back toward the river. Just past the Bancroft, an abandoned six-story building of blacked-out windows loomed on the river's edge. The river itself was a dark grey scar cutting through the city.

"You cool with everything that went down tonight?" Heywood asked, handing me the blunt again.

I waved off the hit. "I'm all right." I'd gone back into the coffee shop to talk to Bruce. He wouldn't budge. No more poetry nights. Period. While I was trying to reason with him, Joshua was moving from Jimmy Buffet into Simon and Garfunkel and then into Cat Stevens. Most of the people who had shown up for the open mic had left, their seats taken over by people coming in off the street—people who were buying coffee and scones, talking, and singing along with the music.

Coyote had stayed, scribbling on napkins and howling between songs.

Bruce made a move to get behind the counter to help his barista.

I pointed toward Joshua. "I'm gonna grab my mic and amplifier as soon as he takes a break."

Bruce gave me a disappointed look. His voice was quiet. "Whatever you have to do, Denver," he sighed, shrugging and walking off to get behind the counter.

The whole place was different with the music. Nobody seemed uneasy or annoyed as they had been during the poetry. They were chattering at their tables. Smiling. Some were mouthing the words to the songs or singing along. Joshua was doing nothing but cover tunes I'd heard from dozens of other guys in coffee shops or bars. In Ann Arbor, every place had its version of Joshua, if not two. Nothing obscure from them. No B-side shit. Like all those other guys, Joshua knew his audience. It's what they wanted—the familiar. Don't try to take me anywhere that I haven't already been, their smiling faces were saying. Give me Margaritaville. Give me Julio down in the schoolyard. Give me moon shadows or peace trains. Don't try to show me the world in a way I haven't already seen it. Sing the words that are so well-known that we don't even have to listen to them. Hell, who wants to think about the words?

Wasn't Cat Stevens saying something about "the world as one?" Ah shit, who cares, I just do the clapping part.

Sing us the old songs, their happy faces said, sing us the lyrics that are like old friends.

Keep your damn poetry to yourself, weirdo.

Joshua finished up "Yellow Submarine." He smiled. "I'm going to take a quick fifteen minute break," he said. "I'll be right back."

I started toward the microphone and amp, feeling a little like that kid that says he's just going to take his ball and go home.

Joshua stopped me and shook my hand. "Hey, man, thanks a lot," he said. He told me Bruce was going to pay him thirty bucks every Thursday night to play, plus tips. "He said he might try Tuesday nights, too. He's calling it Jams with Joshua."

"Great," I said.

He smiled and clamped his hand on my shoulder and shook me. "No kidding, dude. It wouldn't have happened without you."

I looked into his face. "Why…because I shot off my big mouth?"

His face went warm and kind. "No, man, because you started the open mic in the first place. There wasn't anything like it going on in Old Town in a long time. I've been trying to get a gig like this for over a year." Thanking me again, he squeezed his sweaty hand on my shoulder, then walked off to receive the half-priced, complimentary coffee that Bruce had waiting for him.

I grabbed the donation bucket. I ended up leaving the mic and amplifier. I figured maybe my dad could drive me in the truck to get them the next day. There wasn't any sense in me raining on Joshua's parade.

Helen came up to me with her scrapbooks tucked under her arm. "I've heard these songs too many times," she said. She pressed something into my hand. "Save that house."

I didn't look at the money until after she left. It was two tens, the most money that had been donated all night. As far as I knew, she was on a fixed income.

"I guess it worked out pretty well for Joshua," I said to Heywood. "He's decent enough."

Covenant Hospital was a spectacle of lit windows on our right.

Heywood nodded toward the campus of pane-lit buildings. "That's where my mama works."

I nodded. It was where my mom was before finally moving into hospice.

Up ahead near the art museum, the lights of a police car flashed blue and red in the windows of the surrounding buildings. He had somebody pulled over.

Heywood pinched out the ember at the end of the blunt and then popped the roach into his mouth. "I'm willing to bet a Benjamin that that car is full of brothers," he said, swallowing.

"I don't even have a quarter to bet."

"Good," he said, "You'd lose it."

We drove by. The cop—a white guy—was leaned down into the driver's window shining a flashlight over the four young, black male faces inside. They squinted, turning their heads, as he moved the light from face to face.

What was it with cops and their lights?

"I called it," Heywood said. "See that? Nice car, too. Niggers like that can't have a nice car. That's what that cop's thinking. They must be doing something wrong, right?" He shook his head. "Man, I hate this fucking city."

I didn't know what to say. I didn't like the city either, but I knew that the red of our anger was different. His ran deeper and from a more beat down place. I wasn't going to pretend that I understood it. I touched my finger along the dashboard above the glove box.

"Could just as easily be a carload of white boys, right?" Heywood held up a finger. "Difference is white boys would actually have to do something to get pulled over. Four black kids like that? Shit, all they have to be is inside a nice car. Crime enough right there."

"That's such bullshit," I said, trying not to sound patronizing. "It's not right."

We drove past the lights of Old Town.

"That's why I have it all right in this piece of shit," Heywood said, patting the steering wheel. "I drive by a cop in this car and he thinks, 'yup, that's about right. That's the kind of car he should be in.'" He laughed. "You think if I had the money, I'd buy a nice car?"

I guessed that I knew what he was driving at. "No," I said.

"No? Why, no? Why the fuck can't I have a nice car if I got bank?"

Anything good I'd been feeling from the weed was going fast. "Heywood—"

He laughed. "Don't mind me, man. I'm getting all wack on your ass. Just this place…sometimes it fucks you up. I hate it here— leastways hate a lot of the people, na mean?"

I had nothing for him. Thinking of one of levy's poems, I slipped the little book from my back pocket. I could just make out the words in the dash light. It was from his poem, "Cleveland Undercovers," something he'd written about the place, a city he hated and wanted to love, or loved and wanted to keep from hating:

> my god eye seems to have
> no city to see,
> i look into the mind of it
> and smile knowing
> it is young and becoming one
> so it doesn't matter IF or WHY,
> i still have a city to cover with
> > lines…

Heywood thought for a moment and then made a noise in his throat as though what I'd said was gospel. "I hear ya," he said. "Ain't nothing to do but write about it…that's what you're saying?"

I told him I didn't know what I was saying. "That's what this poet, d.a. levy, was saying about Cleveland back in the Sixties. He hated the place, but I think he loved it, too—loved it enough anyway to try to write about it."

Heywood scratched the back of his neck. "So, write about Saginaw?"

"Shit, I don't know. levy was watching all the poets around him take off for California because it seemed like that was the place to be, but levy acted like he could help to make Cleveland the place to be. For him, he used poetry. Said things as true as he could, like your poem about your brother." I shrugged. "Getting it out there…saying what happened and trying to get people to listen. Saying it true, right?"

He nodded. "Mm hmm."

I looked at him. "You ever read 'Sonny's Blues' by James Baldwin?"

He shook his head. "That a poem?"

"No, a short story about these two brothers in Harlem. It's got this part in it about how music, poetry…any of it. None of it can really say anything new. All of it's been said, right? Still, we got to keep saying it. Maybe until somebody actually listens."

Heywood drove. His face looked thoughtful.

"You should really read some Baldwin. Big writer in his day— African American. You'd like him." Then I thought about what I'd just said and shook my head. "I'm sorry, man."

"What the hell you talking about?"

We passed the poorly-lit storefronts of struggling restaurants and vacant businesses.

"I don't know…telling you that you should read Baldwin because he's black? That just seems a little racist, like I'm not much better than that cop back there."

Heywood burst out laughing.

"What?"

He shook his head and fished a Black and Mild out of his pocket. "You think too much, DH. I'm surprised your head don't blow up." He flicked up a flame and talked around the cigar. "If that's what college does for you, you can have it."

He laughed and lit his cigar. "Anyway man, it's time I drop your ass back in the township. I gotta get over to my girl's. She'll lock the door on me if I'm too late. Be a shame for her to miss out on what I have for her."

"I hear you." I knew what he was talking about. It made me think about Heather.

He turned off of Brockway onto Center. "That poet you were talking about. levy. He sound deep."

I told him about how everything—fighting it all the time— wore levy down. He gave up on words and started doing concrete poetry. His friends were taking off. It was looking likely that he was going to do more jail time. It was all too much, and he lifted that rifle down.

"Damn," Heywood whispered.

I flipped to another poem:

cleveland, i gave you
the poems that no one ever
wrote about you
and you gave me
NOTHING…
cleveland, I gave you
poems that no one else had time
to write
& you arrested me
AND I DON'T EVEN CARE

in the days unborn
you will find my brothers
ARMED with words you havent
even dreamed of

Heywood took a drag and exhaled out his window. "Maybe that's you and me, man."

I laughed. "Well, you maybe. Not me. I don't know if I know anything about poetry. I feel pretty dried up, you know?"

Heywood cleared his throat. "You ain't dried up to me," he said. "Shit, man, I don't know…I'm always thinking, this white boy talks some real talk. Gets my head on fire, you know?"

I pinched my thumb against my finger and pressed them to my lips. I mimicked taking a hit off the blunt. "You put a nice little fire in my brain, too."

He pointed the cigar at me. "I ain't frontin'. Shit, you got me to read a poem in public…least some of a poem. Writing poetry… you keep that shit to yourself in my neighborhood, like AIDS. Nobody wants to hear it. Nobody listens."

What he was saying reminded me of a night in Professor Seager's class. He was one of U of M's biggest poets—older guy with thinning gray hair and seven books to his name. It took me two years of trying to register before I finally got into one of his workshops. I remember that we had finished up a really great night of workshopping near the end of the semester. We were all a little high on it—a little high on being poets—and a little ready to head out to the bar and drink and talk poetry. Seager told us he had one more thing to say before we left. He looked tired, exhaling into the fingers he'd brought to his lips. "What we've been doing in here all semester, what we did tonight…it isn't exactly real, now is it?"

The whole room got quiet. "You bring your poems in, and sometimes they're not so great (nervous laughter), and we listen to them, and talk about them, and give them more time than they deserve. For a solid half hour, your poetry has an attentive audience…hell, a vested audience." He pointed to the door. "It's not like that out there. It's not. Nobody is going to give a damn. You'll be an anomaly in your families. Maybe even an embarrassment. You're going to have to fight…What we're doing in here, it's a deceptive thing. It probably has all of you thinking…believing that the rest of the world—" Then he just stopped. He looked at our faces and just stopped. He started laughing. "Don't listen to me. Not tonight, don't listen. As far as I can tell, I'm intruding into bar time (more laughter). I remember those nights." He raised his arm. "Have one for me. Hell, I'd go with you if the doctor didn't give me so much shit about drinking." We all laughed.

Everybody was pretty quiet for the first half hour at the bar. Then, the beer kicked in. We were writers and poets again. Seager's words were just a nuisance. We were drunk poets, and Seager was easy to forget. He was just an old man. What did he know?

"Take a left up here, just past the Red Horse bar," I told Heywood. "That's my street." A red Pegasus looked ready for flight on the side of the building. "That poem you started to read tonight—'Red Streets'—it's a good poem, man." I pointed to my driveway. "Here," I said.

He slid the car into park and held up his hand. I grasped it in mine, closing my hand around the base of his thumb as he did the same to mine. What surprised me was when he pulled me in for a one-shoulder hug and clapped me on the back. "Thanks, DH. Stay peace."

I told him to do the same.

I stood in the driveway and watched his taillights until they flashed red and then disappeared when he turned left into the traffic of State Street. He was something I'd never really associated with Saginaw.

A friend.

In high school, I wasn't one of those genius students who excelled in every subject and took honors classes. English was my thing, and most of my classmates rated English as their least favorite subject. My shyness usually damned me to having my nose in a book, which got me labeled as some kind of academic snob, which the top students knew not to be true. I wasn't taking the physics course or the calculus course or Advanced Chemistry...I was just a glitch in the AP English classes.

The slackers didn't claim me. The brains didn't claim me. The burners, the jocks, the punks...none of them claimed me. Most didn't even know my name.

Heywood called me DH. I liked that.

In the distance, two people—a man and a woman—were yelling at each other in the Red Horse's parking lot. After a moment, a Harley Davidson fired up and roared off into the night. "Go to hell, you sonuvabitch!" the woman screamed. I listened to the motorcycle until its sound faded away.

Taking a few steps, I stood in my father's front yard, much the same way I'd stood in the yard at the Roethke House. The place was dark except for the faint light glowing through the drawn blinds of the front window. Dad's lamp. He hadn't gone to bed yet. I looked at the door. I breathed in then exhaled a long breath.

The rider out there somewhere free on his Harley.

7.

Turning the cold knob, I eased the door open, slipped into the house, and closed the door behind me. On the radio, two commentators were doing a post-game wrap-up. It sounded like the Tigers had lost: "The top of the lineup isn't connecting the way they need to. It's a shame too because Boesch has been pretty consistent with doubles and even a few triples in the cleanup slot."

I locked the deadbolt and then whispered the chain into place, sneaking into the house as soundlessly as I'd slipped out of it back in high school days to take late-night walks.

I looked at my dad sleeping in the halo of lamp light. My plan was to sneak past him and into the basement. Somehow, though, I ended up next to his chair standing over him. I reached down to turn out the light. He'd gotten so old. His hair had been white for the last ten years. I could see where it was beginning to thin in the swirl of the crown. The skin of his face sagged, and his hands were freckled with age spots. Two of his knuckles had split open and then healed over into oily scabs. His hands, always in some stage of healing, were a testimony to the way he threw himself into household repairs.

Work. It was always work with him.

When I was young, he tried to teach me how to fix things. More often than not, fifteen minutes into a project, he would look at me and say, "You can go." What a relief those words were. Released, I would retreat up to my room to get back into whatever novel I was reading.

Books confirmed what I had always felt anyway. Life is a damn hard game when you really begin to think about the rules, especially when the rules seem absurd and you want, more than anything, to play the game differently. Everyone else, though, seems satisfied with the rules and wants, more than anything, for you to just shut up and play the game.

When I was holed up in my room, my reading was always soundtracked by my father's work coming up through the cold air return: hammering, drilling, sanding. Sometimes, listening to him, I had wished that I could be more like him. He played by the rules and never really questioned the game. He saw the world in pretty simple terms. It's a place where things break or wear out. It's a place that asks you to get off your ass and do something about it. You work, or you watch the things around you—the things that you love, or at least the things that you call yours—slowly erode. His was a life about fighting the erosion and not really worrying about whether or not the fight was worthwhile.

He wasn't a bad dad, not really. He was always trying to include me. He had things to teach a son, at least a son who was willing to listen and wanted to know more about tools. There were so many kids that I went to high school with—kids whose dads ignored them or weren't around at all—who would have thrived with Lee Hoptner for a father.

I wished that son could have been me. I just wasn't, though.

I studied him, looking pale and exhausted. His breathing was shallow, and he didn't smell good. His shirt was dark with sweat under each armpit. I wondered if maybe he was ill. As much as I wanted to let that sleeping dog lie, I couldn't. He needed to be in bed.

I put my hand on his shoulder, its thinness surprising me, and jostled him. "Dad, you should probably head upstairs."

He made a noise, but his eyes didn't open.

I jostled again. "Wake up, Dad. You're going to get a kink in your neck if you sleep like that."

He opened his eyes and squinted in the light. "Did I fall asleep? What time is it?" he asked through the yawn

"I don't know, probably around eleven. It's late."

He rubbed his eyes and adjusted himself in the chair. Rolling his shoulder in its socket, he massaged it. "How was your thing?"

I sighed. "Went about as well as anything has been going for me lately."

He pinched his sweaty shirt away from his sternum and shook it. "It's hot. Why don't you grab us each a beer?"

I went into the kitchen and came back with the beers. We cracked them open.

Dad turned off the radio. "Sounds like the Tigers lost."

"You didn't listen to the game?"

"On and off." He took a sip and then lowered his can. "You didn't get many people tonight?"

I shrugged. "There were people. I don't know. I guess I just don't want to do it anymore. It's too much work." I regretted saying the last part as soon as it came out. He was going to jump all over it…more evidence of me and my aversion to effort.

He switched his beer to his other hand and then back again. "Seems you were pretty excited about those open mics a couple weeks ago."

I squeezed my eyes closed and pinched the bridge of my nose. He'd been awake for five minutes, and he was already looking for an argument. "Look, Dad, it's just a waste of my time, okay? Same people show up. Same shitty poems. It's just not worth it."

He made a clicking sound in his cheek. "You really think you should quit something before you even—"

"Dad, seriously, just let it go. Jesus Christ, it's not that big of a deal."

He held up a hand in surrender. "I was just asking." He took a pull of his beer. "You know about this stuff better than I do. Who the hell am I to say anything about an open mic, right? " He smiled.

Open mic. It was a phrase that he probably never guessed that he would use in his life. I didn't know why I lied to him. Why not just tell him about what had happened between Bruce and me? In the end, he would have told me that I shouldn't have lost my head the way I did. It was a coffee shop, not a poetry shop. Customer orders an espresso, you make the espresso. "You pay attention to the guy with the money," I imagined him saying, "not the guy with the poem, Denver."

Either way, the truth or a lie, we would have ended up harping at each other. We always did.

I set my beer on my knee, ready to make him happy. "I thought it over tonight," I said. "I'm going to go to that interview on Monday." It seemed like the right time to extend an olive branch. I smiled.

He nodded and then took a drink of his beer. He looked me in the face. "That'd be good."

That'd be good? That's all I got. Even when I finally did what he wanted me to do, it wasn't enough.

I stood up and held the beer can out toward him. "I'm going to finish this downstairs."

"Upstairs," he said.

I stopped mid-step. "What?"

He set his beer on the table, crossed his arms, and looked at me. "I moved you out of the basement and set you up in the guest room."

I numbed at the news. "Wha...Why?" I shook my head. "Why the hell do you do stuff like that, Dad?"

He picked up his beer can and lifted it towards his mouth. One of his fingers came off of the can and pointed at me. "Because it needed to be done," he said, just before taking a drink.

I crossed my arms. Something hot was working just under my skin like electricity. "Oh, okay, so let me guess…it needed to be done, and I'm too lazy to do it. That's it, isn't it?"

"You're saying that, not me."

Out on the street, a motorcycle roared past, ripping up the silence. They'd be pulling out of the Red Horse for the next two hours. I had to wait until the noise died off.

I took a step toward him. "Fine," I said, "you're not saying it, but you're thinking it. You've always thought it." I pointed a finger at him from the same hand that was holding my beer. Some of it sloshed from the hole and landed on the carpet.

He looked down at the spot where the beer disappeared. Then he looked up at me again. "You want to take it easy?" He pushed himself to standing.

I swallowed and took a step back from him. "You really had no right to move my stuff, you know."

He said that he never thought of me as lazy. "Stubborn, though. Good goddamn are you stubborn." He smiled and shook his head.

Stubborn?

"Don't look at me like that. Don't act surprised like you can't understand what I'm talking about. Your mother must have told me a thousand times that you can't be lazy and get the grades that you were getting. She wore me down on that front." He told me that he had to figure out some other reason why I never did one thing that he told me to do. "That's the only thing I could come up with. You're stubborn, especially toward me. If I say it or suggest it, you're going to say no, even if it's the best thing for you."

"It's my stuff," I said, having nothing else.

He laughed. "I know it's your stuff. Your stuff sitting down in a damp, leaky basement. Your books—all five hundred pounds of them—sitting down there getting ready to go moldy. I could already smell funk on them." He asked me what I would have done if he had suggested that we move me into the guestroom.

"I—"

"No," he said, shaking his head, "don't answer. I already know the answer. I already heard it from you earlier today when I made the same goddamn suggestion. You say it every time like clockwork. 'I'm fine, Dad,'" he said, in a mocking, affected voice. "You're always fine. Hell, you could have a broken leg, and if I said, 'Hey, maybe we should get a cast on that,' you'd say, 'I'm fine.' Then you'd let it heal all twisted as hell and go around with a gimp just to stick it to me." He took a few limping steps to show me.

Sweat welled up across my forehead. "Look, Dad—"

He pointed at me. "You're so pig-headed, I can't believe...I mean, just now, when you told me that you were going to go to that interview, you were looking at me like I was supposed to start jumping up and down. Like I owe you thanks for sticking my neck out for you. You got it turned around in your head that you're actually doing me a favor. Is that the only way you can stomach it?" He looked at me, waiting for an answer. "You can't stand the idea of having to thank me, can you?"

I couldn't move or speak. It was like someone shot novocaine through my veins. He was right. Damn it, he was right.

He shook his head. "Unbelievable. You know what? I'm done here." He picked his beer up from the table.

I found my voice. "I'm sorry. I didn't—"

"Forget it," he said, walking past me and waving me off with his hand.

"Dad, I'm trying to thank you, here."

He spun around. "It's too late, Denver. I don't want to hear it now, okay? It shouldn't be that much work."

"Dad—"

He turned back toward the kitchen. "Do whatever you want to do. Bring all your stuff back to the basement. Piss on the interview. I don't give a shit, anymore."

"I already said—"

"I'm getting too old for this. I'm tired of fighting." He walked off into the kitchen. The patio door slid open and then closed again.

I stood for awhile in the living room, taking in long breaths and then exhaling. I didn't understand what had happened. Through the patio door, I could see his silhouette standing in the yard.

I thought of him moving all of my stuff up two flights of stairs. I felt guilty. Just as quickly, I was angry. Why couldn't he just leave it alone?

I went upstairs. The guestroom was a replica of what I had set up down in the basement. The reading lamp that he put on a table next to my bed was on. I didn't know how he did it, maybe with a dolly and straps, but he even got my desk up the stairs. Before coming up, I had imagined the work of putting all of my books away. I had imagined piles on the floor.

Even that, though, he had done. All of them were put away on my mother's old bookshelves. He must have worked from the moment I left the house. It was the only way to get it all done on his own before I got home.

A telephone was on the desk. I dropped back into the chair and picked up the receiver. The dial tone droned. I listened to it for a little bit—its emptiness—and then punched in the number.

Heather answered. Her voice gave nothing away. People were talking behind her. It didn't sound loud enough to be a bar. Some kind of small gathering. I could hear guys talking. Laughing.

"What's going on?" I asked.

"I'm with people." This time I heard it in her tone. She was wishing that she had let me go to voicemail. Then she could have deleted me without listening.

"You having fun?" I asked.

"Yup."

Why did I call her? I toyed with the idea of just hanging up. "I just got back from that open mic I've been hosting."

"Yeah?" I could almost see her rolling her eyes. "How was it?"

I started to tell her about Heywood and his poetry. "You'd like him. He's different from the people we were in school with. He's really down to earth."

"I liked the people we went to school with just fine."

I told her that I did, too. "Heywood's different, though. Not so full of himself...you know, like some poets can be." I launched into the story of Heywood's reading and the mess with the espresso machine.

She opened up to the conversation a little. "That is exactly the reason that I will never do a coffee shop reading again."

I nodded. "No kidding, right? This guy who owns the shop is a real douche—"

"Denver, why are you calling me?"

I swallowed. "I don't know...just to talk. I wanted to tell you about—"

"You said you didn't want to talk to me anymore. You said you didn't want to hear me bragging."

"I was just in a pissy mood, you know?"

She told me that it was probably a good idea that we don't talk for awhile.

I pushed my hand through my hair and squeezed the top of my head. "Okay. That's fine. I mean, if that's the way you feel."

"It is," she said. Then she hung up.

I set the phone back in its cradle and went over to the shelves. I didn't have to look at the books for long to see that my dad had put them away in the exact order I'd had them on the shelves down in the basement.

Jesus Christ.

"If you're going to do a job, you might as well take the time to get the details right." That was one of his favorite lines.

I knelt down and slid *Rabbit, Run* free from the others. I flipped the pages and smelled the hint of mustiness in them. I rubbed my eyes.

Every book. Exactly where I'd had it.

Standing up, I walked over to the window. When I was a kid, this was my room. For a long time it didn't even have a way to look outside or let sunlight in. Dad said that was no way for a kid to grow up. He added a dormer and a window. I really didn't remember ever looking outside. He probably thought I ignored the window to spite him. I was always on my bed. Always reading. I didn't have any use for looking outside.

The neighbor's roofs were triangles of black shadows. Beneath them, scattered squares of light out in the residential darkness. The sky was blue-black with overcast. More storms were coming. A weatherman had talked about it.

June rains.

My dad's mind was probably on the basement, the water that would come in, dampening like a lost son returning.

I looked down. His silhouette was still there in the yard. Just standing there.

A small orange ember hovered next to him, then floated up to his mouth. Third cigarette of the day, at least.

8.

"It ain't a fucking race."

Mop in my sore hand, I turned and looked across the roof toward Ricky, my co-worker of two weeks. Squinting, I could just make him out in all the sunlight reflecting off the metal around him. He was sitting on an upside down five-gallon bucket. After a week and a half of painting rooms inside, we'd been recoating the hotel's flat roofs with a silvery goop for the last three days. My feet were sweating in a pair of old snow boots that my dad let me use for the job. They looked like they were covered in mercury or aluminum. The blisters on my hands had already burst and were raw and stinging against the mop handle. I stood taller and stretched my aching lower back.

"Take a break, College," Ricky said.

That was his name for me. College. I'd made the mistake of telling him that I graduated from Michigan. He found the whole thing pretty funny. "You with a degree, and we're both up here sweating our balls off and slopping silvercoat side by side. And, I'm making a buck more an hour than you to boot," he laughed. "I always knew college was a fucking waste of time."

I wasn't sure that I could argue with him. The week before I'd received a letter. They were still forwarding my mail from Ann Arbor. The letter was from a magazine out in California called *The Activerse*. Their submissions guidelines said they wanted poems that advocated making the world a better place. They wanted words that could inspire action. They'd had some poems of mine for eight months. I'd figured they'd been lost.

I wished they had been.

The editor left a hand-written note on the rejection letter. He said that they really liked the spirit of what I was trying to say. "These read like tiny essays, though, not poems," he wrote. "Does your local college offer any poetry writing courses that you could take just to get some of the basics?"

A good kick to the proverbial kidneys.

I set my mop handle down and worked my way around a colossal, humming air conditioning unit to get to Ricky.

When I did, he told me that his wife had just texted him. "She knows when my breaks are," he said.

Ricky was probably about thirty years old. He had red hair, a patchy-looking red beard, freckled arms, and a pale gut that was peeking out from under his untucked shirt. He took a drag from a cigarette, exhaled and then, with his other hand, took a bite out of a sandwich. A meatball squeezed out the back end of the sub and splattered on a part of the roof that we'd finished the day before. Ricky looked, then nudged the meatball under the air conditioning unit with his boot.

He always had food. He carried a small, red cooler with him, which was open next to his feet, revealing another long sub sandwich wrapped in aluminum foil, a Tupperware filled with what looked like macaroni and cheese, and three Mountain Dews.

"Check it out," he said. He held the screen of his phone toward me so I could read it:

Come home I am in bed naked

"I'm gonna ask her with who…the mailman or the UPS guy?" he said, laughing. His open mouth was a mess of red sauce, meat, and masticated white bread.

"I'm going down to the break room," I said. "I need to get out of the sun for awhile."

Not saying anything, he set his sandwich on the knee of his filthy pants and started pressing in a message. His beat-up, silver-flecked thumbs looked huge on the tiny keyboard. He was laughing to himself.

I stood by the edge of the roof next to the top of the extension ladder. The ground was some thirty feet below. As it had been since we started, my stomach did a little twist. Still, I wanted to be able to do it. Ricky went up and down the ladder like it was a flight of stairs. Nothing to it, for him.

Taking a few breaths, I turned my back to the edge, grabbed the sides of the ladder's top, and tried to lower my right foot to a rung. I closed my eyes and waited for my boot to find something solid. I reached, didn't touch anything, then lifted my foot back to the edge. I did it again. Then again. Every time I tried, I pictured the bottom of the ladder slipping and me plummeting to the sidewalk below. My heart raced.

Ricky was still mashing a message into his phone. Glancing up, he looked over at me and shook his head. He set his sandwich on top of the air conditioning unit and walked my way. He was shaking his head, but smiling. "Jesus Christ, College, I told you you ain't gonna fall."

I shrugged.

He held the top of the ladder. It wasn't as good as somebody holding it from the bottom, but it was enough that I could swing myself onto it and get both feet on the rungs. Ricky and I were making progress. He didn't even give the ladder a little shake when I was halfway down, which had been his running joke.

I waved up to him from the sidewalk, and his head disappeared. Unbuckling the snow boots, I changed into my tennis shoes which I'd left in the bushes next to the ladder.

Once down in the hotel's basement, I almost went into the break room, but the laundry maid was in there smoking, so I sneaked past. Shirley was nearing sixty, overweight, and had a cigarette-sanded voice. She stood in a room all day with three gigantic washers and three gigantic dryers. The drone and bang of it was awful. For eight hours, she washed, dried, and folded pillow cases, sheets, wash cloths and towels. The varicose veins in her legs looked like purple raisins lodged under her skin.

It must have been lonely work because when she got to the break room, she liked to talk. She had a daughter who was having a lot of trouble with her boyfriend, a drinker who kept burning through the little bit of money they had. Shirley thought that her daughter should break things off with the guy. "I see why she don't, though. She got two little kids with him. She wants their daddy to be in their lives," she'd said, using her cigarette to push around a few spent butts in the ashtray.

I didn't really mind all that much listening to Shirley. She was nice enough, and seemed to really like that someone was hearing her. It was just her chain smoking. The break room wasn't very big. The way she fogged the place in, my eyes would water. They were already bad enough from being up on the roof with all that sun glaring off the silvercoat.

I went and sat at one of the desks in the maintenance shop. Vance, my supervisor, came in a minute later. He was built solid, with small ropes of veins running up and down his forearms. Pretty near bald except for a horseshoe of blonde hair around his head and a tuft in front just above his forehead, he had a walkie talkie on his belt.

He looked at me sitting at the desk doing nothing.

"We're on break," I said.

He nodded. "How are things going up there?"

I told him what Ricky had told me...that we'd probably be done with the roof the next morning. As I shifted in the chair, my lower back felt like clay hardening.

He sat at his desk. "Tomorrow? Good enough, I guess. We need you guys inside as soon as possible."

Brian's voice came out of Vance's walkie talkie. "Vance, we got anymore flappers in the shop?"

I always smiled when I heard them talking about flappers, thinking of a bunch of women with bobbed hair and short skirts stored away in a cabinet of the shop somewhere. I imagined opening the door to them all brandishing cigarette holders and asking me for a light.

Vance radioed back. "Just got a shipment this morning."

I grinned again, picturing a box with air holes—smoke and jazz leaking from them.

Of the interviews I'd been on, my interview with Vance had been the most unusual. He hardly even looked at my résumé.

"A degree in poetry?" He scratched his temple and smiled. "Man, what a country."

I shrugged.

He slapped his hand on the table. "You don't know a damn thing about hotel maintenance, do you?" he said, laughing.

I admitted that I didn't. At least he didn't ask me what I thought my future in maintenance would be.

"Well, I'm going to hire you." He smiled. "You want to know why?"

I shrugged. "Because of my dad?"

He shook his head. "Nope. For three reasons. First, you were on time. That's big in my book. Two, you take things seriously. Hell, you even wore a tie and a jacket. And three, you don't stink of booze, which is a lot more than I can say for the other guy I interviewed this morning.

"No matter how much they know, they're useless to me if they won't work." He shook his head. "Had a guy here this winter that could fix anything." Vance's hand swept through the air in front of him. "Anything. What he liked to fix most, though, were rum and Cokes. I caught him on his lunch break at the bar across the street. He didn't even flinch when I walked in, like he was waiting for me. I sat down on the stool next to him, ordered him another round, and told him to consider it severance pay."

I didn't know how I was supposed to respond to the story. I shook my head and made a little noise of disbelief in the back of my throat.

"Your old man probably told you that it's a temporary position, right? I'll need you for about a month. After that, we'll see." He said that some of the guys would be taking their vacations in August, and that I could probably fill in for them.

He stood up and told me that he was going to be right back with a W-4 form. "I have a uniform in the shop that should fit you."

I swallowed. "I'm starting today?"

He looked at me with hard eyes. "Is that a problem?"

I shook my head.

"Good answer." He explained that in a month the hotel was going to be hosting an important conference. "Some big insurance company out of Detroit. The hotel manager is hoping to land more conferences of the same size, so he wants everything to be perfect."

That ended the interview. Ten minutes later, I was uniformed and learning how to cut in with a paintbrush.

Picking silvercoat from my fingernails, I looked at the clock. Four minutes left of break. Vance was bent over some papers at his desk. He looked over to a calculator, banged in some numbers, and then looked back at the papers. I stretched my hands open in front of my face and studied the oily, split-open blisters.

I'd met up with Heywood at the Schuch bar the night before. I was tired, but I'd already canceled on him twice the previous week. He wanted me to look at a new poem. I told him about my plan instead. My first roommate from the dorms, a film major, had emailed me. He was living out in Portland, Oregon since graduating. He was working freelance for an advertising company and trying to make a short film on the side. I told him about my situation in Saginaw, especially with my old man. He emailed back and said that he could use a roommate and that I was welcome to come out. Portland was supposed to be a cool city. I'd learned a lot about painting since working at the hotel. I figured I could get on a painting crew once I got out there. If I hitchhiked, I would arrive with close to six hundred dollars in my pocket. It'd be enough to get me started. Saginaw was hollowing me out.

Vance cleared his throat. "I write some poetry, too."

I looked over at him scratching his fingers into his goatee and looking at me, smiling.

He shrugged and looked down at his papers. "Mainly during deer season. I bring some paper and a pen out in the blind with me. I'll bring one in some time. You can tell me if it's any good."

I shrugged and nodded. I could only imagine one of his poems:

> Raised my gun, aimed at his head,
> pulled the trigger…
> that buck's fucking dead.

"I should probably get back up to the roof," I said, standing up. I groaned as I straightened my stiff back.

He smiled. "I wasn't sure how you were going to work out, but you're doing fine. You got hustle. You're the only guy I have that doesn't need twenty-five minutes to take a fifteen-minute break."

Something good washed through me. It was probably the first time anyone had ever complimented my work ethic. "Thanks," I said.

"Maybe you'll rub off on Ricky. Between his cigarettes and his texting..." He shook his head and snorted a laugh. "And then his bowels. He can turn a shit into a symphony if it means more time away from work."

Laughing, I started for the door.

"Hold on," he said, pinching his nose between a thumb and forefinger. "Let me tell you something." He turned and set his hands on his knees. Then he brought his palms together and worried them against each other. "I remember when I started in maintenance at a hotel over in Bay City. I was eighteen or so. It was in the winter and we had this huge snowstorm. The snow just kept coming and coming...you know, off the lake like it does. I couldn't do much of anything when I started, but I could shovel. That's what I did. I kept this long sidewalk in front of the hotel free of snow. I'd get done shoveling it, turn around, and start shoveling it again. I must have been out there for five hours. My supervisor came out and told me that he'd been watching me work. He said, 'You're going to make it.' Then he went back inside."

Vance smiled at me. "That's what I think when I watch you work. I know you don't know much, but you throw yourself into what you're doing." He nodded. "I've been waiting to drop that same line on someone, someone young like I was back then. It's good to hear that stuff. So, let me just tell you...I think you're going to make it, too."

I smiled. Maybe I even blushed. "Thanks, Vance."

He nodded and then turned back to the papers on his desk. "If you get the chance, toss Ricky's phone over the edge, will ya?"

I told him that I would. Walking down the hallway past the break room and up the stairs to the lobby, I felt a little bad that I'd dismissed the idea of Vance writing poetry. He was a good guy. Maybe he wrote good poems.

Standing at the bottom of the ladder, I shouted for Ricky. When his face didn't appear, I shouted for him again.

He looked over the edge and shook his head. "Oh my god, College. Would you stop being such a pussy fart."

"Just hold the ladder."

He stood for a moment. "Wait a second," he yelled, probably finishing up a text or the last bites of that second sandwich. It wasn't long before his gloved hands were on either side of the top of the ladder.

"Okay," he shouted, "come on up."

I climbed up almost to the top where I could see Ricky standing five feet back from the edge of the roof with his hands in his pockets. I looked at the ladder. He had set a glove on either side of it, empty fingers holding it for me.

I scrambled up the rest of the way and onto the roof.

"Well, you finally did it, College."

"That was bullshit, man."

He laughed. "Shit, it's what you needed. You think too fucking much."

I stared at him.

"It's like when you're with your lady," he said. "You start thinking about it, and you're going to shoot your wad soon as you put your sword in the sheath." He made a squirting sound with his lips and teeth.

Still, I didn't crack a smile.

"Oh, would you just relax, for Christsake." He turned and started towards the buckets.

We worked silently for a few minutes, plunging the mops, then spreading the silvercoat. It wasn't long before I wasn't angry anymore. I was thinking about how I'd gone up the ladder and it never once felt unsteady.

Sword in the sheath, I thought, smiling. What a metaphor.

The sun had gone behind some clouds, and a breeze was blowing over the roof. It was a good time of the day. I could still hear the way Vance had said it: "You got hustle."

"You ever had a problem with that?" Ricky asked. He leaned on his mop handle and fit a cigarette between his lips.

"What?"

"You know what I'm talking about...your wad jumping the gun." He lit his cigarette.

I shrugged.

He took a drag. "My buddy said to think about triangles. Think about a big triangle and little triangles going through it." He closed his eyes. "Just close your eyes and think about triangles."

I kept pushing my mop. "That work? The triangles?"

He exhaled a cloud of smoke. "Fuck no."

After a minute, I told him about a yoga course I took to fulfill my PE requirement at Michigan. Sixteen women in it, and two guys, me and an Art History major. The teacher took the two of us aside after class about a month and a half into the semester. We'd just learned how touching your tongue to the roof of your mouth can connect the front and back channels of energy in your body, allowing cooler energy through the third eye. He told us we can do it during sex, too. "Just touch your tongue to the hard palette and turn it in circles. You'll last as long as she needs you to."

It probably was the best thing I learned in college. Hell, maybe it was part of the reason Heather had stayed with me for as long as she did. "It's called Nabho Mudra," I told Ricky.

He looked at me. "That shit works?"

I pushed my mop into the bucket. "Works for me."

"Nabho Mudra," he said dismissively, shaking his head.

At the end of the day, we stood near the edge of the roof and looked back over the sea of silver that we'd spread.

"We finished early," Ricky said. "Vance'll be happy."

The sun was to our backs, throwing our long shadows over the silvercoat. We'd covered what amounted to at least a football field. I couldn't explain it, but the sight of it filled me up with something. Something good. A lot of me was in that roof.

At the Schuch the night before, Heywood had looked put out after I'd told him about Portland. He'd had a folded piece of paper under his hand the whole time I was talking. When I was done, he slipped it back into his shirt pocket.

I pointed. "Is that the poem you brought? I can take a look at it."

He shook his head. "Nah. It ain't much, anyway."

We drank our beers for awhile, not talking. When I finished, I told him that I needed to get going. "I have to be in to work early, and I still need to walk home yet. These twelve-hour days have me whipped."

He nodded toward the bar. "They got a picture of your boy back there."

"What?"

"Roethke."

Roethke? I figured he was mistaken. "I'll check it out." I told him that I'd get in touch with him before I left town.

He only nodded. I'd hoped that he would, but he didn't offer me a ride home.

It was like Heywood said. There was a picture of Roethke behind the bar with his name under it. It was a black and white I'd never seen before. He was in a three-piece suit sitting on the ground with his back leaned against a cracked brick wall. He looked forlorn, haggard...worn down. Still, something about his eyes made him look determined, like a boxer between rounds, like he was saying, "I'm taking a breather, but I'll be getting up again, don't you worry."

"What do you need?" the bartender asked me.

I pointed at the picture. "That's Theodore Roethke."

He nodded. "Yeah. When he lived in Saginaw, this is where he drank."

"The Schuch? I didn't know that."

The bartender looked at the picture and then back at me. He smiled. "You need something to drink?"

"No, I'm heading home." I looked again. "That's a really great shot of him."

The bartender nodded. "The guy's Saginaw's Hemingway," he said, walking off down the bar to where a customer was signaling for a drink.

Saginaw's Hemingway. It was true. Still, only me, him, and about three other people in the city knew it.

Small clicking noises came from Ricky's mouth. Then he gagged.

"Don't swallow it," I said, shaking my head. "Just touch it to the roof of your mouth."

Beyond the hotel's roof, the Saginaw skyline in the distance was washed in the light of the setting sun. The small windows burned gold in the fading light. The silhouettes of the buildings gave nothing away. It could have been any small Midwestern city.

It could have been a place worth something, even.

I thought of Roethke and his house. Of Heywood and the way he'd slipped his poem back into his pocket. Of my father and how I'd really done nothing to ease his loss, his loneliness.

Then I thought of Vance and how he'd said I was going to make it.

And then, I didn't think at all. I just stood looking out over the silver that blended into that distant gold in the tiny eyes of those buildings. Something hummed along my spine and up into my brain. I pressed my tongue to the roof of my mouth and closed my eyes.

I remembered the ladder and Ricky's empty gloves holding me and how I'd climbed.

I could feel it. I could almost see it with my third eye.

I wasn't going to Portland.

I was staying right here in Saginaw.

9.

I was glad for a day off, a little time to cash my first check. My father was still asleep in his chair when I came in from walking down to the bank and back. It was probably ninety degrees outside. The bank was only a few blocks away. My shirt was clinging wet to me like I'd walked for miles.

During the beginning of the week I had worked so much overtime that the hotel manager made Vance send me home early. I had to take the next day off, too. It was either that or I couldn't work Friday, which was when a shipment of flat-screen televisions was supposed to come in. About forty of the rooms still had old, bulky TVs. While the rest of the guys were doing various touch-ups around the hotel, Vance wanted me to change out the old televisions and deliver and program the new ones, so they'd be ready for the conference guests. "I know you can get it done in one day," he said.

Dad looked pale slumped in his chair. The living room felt like it was being pre-heated to cook a frozen pizza. Oscillating back and forth in front of him, a fan pushed around the warm air. Something hit me, this quick premonition that he was gone and I wouldn't be able to wake him. Watching for the rise and fall of his chest, I could barely draw a breath of my own.

Instead of breathing, he blinked his eyes open and looked at me.

"What? What are you staring at?"

I took a relieved breath and shook my head. "Nothing. I just went down to the bank. I'm back now."

He looked at me as though he could see in my face the way moments before I had feared his death. He turned up the pre-game commentary on the radio. The Tigers had taken a beating on the road. The commentators were recalling some of the more unfortunate games.

"How do you feel, Dad?"

He squinted at me. "What the hell are you talking about?"

I shrugged. "I don't know. You're sleeping a lot."

"Well, I'm tired a lot. I mowed the front lawn yesterday. Back lawn this morning."

I told him that I would have done it.

"This morning I didn't know that you were going to have the afternoon off. It was getting too long back there."

I reminded him that the job ended the next week and that I'd be able to pitch in a little more. Then I fished the bank envelope from my back pocket and peeled it open along its adhesive with my sweaty fingers. Drawing out a hundred dollar bill, I presented it to him. "Even if I'm not around much right now, I can still help out." I smiled. "Here, for rent...or for food or whatever."

He looked at the bill and then up at me. His eyes were thinking. He shook his head and held up his hand. "I'm not going to take this, Denver."

"What? Dad, you said—"

"I don't need it that bad. You have this temporary job. That's your money. It gives you a little pocket dough while you're looking for a new job."

I shook the bill. "Just take it. I mean, the food I've been eating and—"

He held up his palm again. "Just put the money away, Denver. Forget what I said. I'm doing fine. If you get something permanent and you want to stay living here for awhile, then we'll talk about some kind of rent." He shifted and turned up the volume on the radio. "Now let's see what these guys think the Tigers need to do to come out of their slump. They always got a lot of backseat wisdom to share."

I slid the hundred back into the envelope and sat on the couch. I planned to walk to the Roethke House to see if Abby Waters was around. I still had forty bucks that I needed to give her from the fund raiser I'd done at the coffee shop. It wasn't much, but it was something. It certainly wasn't mine to keep.

"No," Dad said, looking at the radio as though he was having a conversation with it. He shook his head. "It's not the hitting. It's the goddamn bullpen." He looked at me, shrugging his hand into the air. "Once the starters are spent, they have nobody to turn to. That whole bullpen is bush league."

I nodded. Sweat dripped from the back of my head and down my neck, tepid little rivulets. "Holy shit, it's hot in here."

He rested his hands on the arms of his chair and leaned his head back. "Trick is not to move much. Then it's not bad." He closed his eyes. The fan ruffled his hair.

I looked at the little radio. It was the same one we used to listen to out in the garage when I was a kid. Even with the antennae up and a ball of aluminum foil cinched around the end, it brought the station in under a hissy whisper of static. "Dad, why don't you let me buy you a flat screen television with the—"

Eyes closed, he started shaking his head.

"No, it wouldn't be for…I mean, it'd be mine, but you could watch the games on it. It'd be like my contribution to the—"

He opened his eyes and looked at me. "I don't want a television in the house, okay?"

I crossed my arms and slumped back against the couch, exhaling. "Alright," I said. There must have been psychology at work, like he wasn't ready to trade roles with me. In his book, he was the provider. He always had been. I was the receiver. It didn't sit well with him to see me offering rent or televisions or anything else. If he didn't accept anything from me, then he didn't have to accept his aging body or his daytime sleepiness. Still, this was my rite of passage, too, wasn't it? I'd taken Anthropology. Didn't he have to allow me the chance to provide? Didn't I need to come of age? Wasn't that part of it, the symbolic acts…be they ritualistic circumcision or the purchasing of a flat-screen television?

Dad sighed, looking at the floor. "I appreciate the offer," he said. "It's just that your mom never wanted a TV in the house." He shrugged his bony shoulders. "I know I could get one, but not having one, I don't know, it's a little like still having her around."

I rubbed the back of my hand across my eyes and blinked. "I miss her, too," I said.

He nodded, squeezing three of the fingers of his left hand in his right. A knuckle cracked. He sat for a moment, watching his hand kneading his fingers. Then he looked at me and forced a smile. "So what are you going to do with your afternoon off? Got big plans? Going to catch up with that Heywood?"

I told Dad all about the Roethke House and the fire and how I'd raised a little money to help them.

"I don't think you're saying that right. I think the h is silent. I'm pretty sure it's pronounced Ret-Key," he said.

I laughed. "I don't think so, Dad."

He shrugged. "Well, in any case, I'm sure they'll appreciate the money." He pulled the arm on his recliner, and the leg-rest lifted his feet. "You can take the truck if you want. Helluva hot day to be walking."

I told him that I still hadn't renewed my license.

He snorted a little laugh and wagged his head side to side.

"I'm going to," I said, smiling. "I will."

The commentators said that the game would be starting soon. The station broke for commercials. Dad turned it down and closed his eyes.

I watched him for a minute, watched his chest rising and falling. When I thought he was asleep, I stood up and started for the door.

"I met him, you know," he said.

I turned. His eyes were still closed. "Met who?"

"Theodore Roethke." He pronounced it Ret-key. Again.

"What do you mean, you met him?"

He opened his eyes and answered while still yawning. "I was about sixteen or seventeen. He came back to Arthur Hill to receive an award, some kind of lifetime achievement thing. A few of us students were invited to the ceremony and got to meet him afterwards."

I reached up under my sleeve and scratched my shoulder. "Just random students?"

He crossed his arms. "No, not just random students. I was there because I wrote this paper on fur trading in the Saginaw Valley." He looked at the radio and touched his finger along the top of it. "And because I'd shown an interest in wanting to teach." He looked back at me.

"To teach?"

Dad nodded. "Yup. Teach history." He was quiet for a moment, touching the radio again. "Anyway, Roethke was a big, gloomy looking sonuvabitch. Dressed like a funeral home director. We all lined up—there were five of us—and he came through and shook our hands and asked a few questions. I remember he stopped when I told him that I wanted to be a teacher. He pointed at my heart. 'Don't give 'em everything,' he said. 'They'll take it. They're hungry.' Then he shook his head. 'If you're doing it right, though, you won't be able to stop giving…even if it's killing you, even if they don't deserve it.' Then he looked at me. 'And, if you're really good— like me—not one of 'em deserves it, not what I give.'"

Dad looked at me. "He was a little full of himself."

"I can't believe you met Roethke," I said, shaking my head.

He took in a breath and exhaled. "I still don't think you're saying it right, Denver."

"Why didn't you ever tell me about meeting him?"

He shrugged. "I didn't really think of it until now."

I sat again on the couch. It was like my dad was a long book, and I was finally getting to some of the good chapters I'd missed. "And you wanting to be a teacher? What happened with that?"

Kneading his fingers again, he took a breath and exhaled. "Grandpa and grandma didn't have the money to send me off to college. Even if they would have, Grandpa didn't want me to go. He couldn't hire anybody, but he couldn't run the store by himself, either. It wasn't a good time for little grocers like him. Bigger stores, like Kessels and Spartan, were popping up around town. He couldn't really compete.

"He let me live at home. He paid me what he could at the end of a week, which wasn't much. Still, it was enough to start saving. And, I was honest with him. I told him that I was saving to go to college." Dad rubbed his eye. "He was good about it, too. He just nodded and didn't argue or say anything about me taking over the store. I think he knew that the store was a lost cause. He was just making what he could until the last of his loyal customers stopped coming through the door."

I knew my dad had worked for GM for a lot of years. By the time I was born, he'd taken early retirement from the plant and was contracting himself out as a handyman. He did everything from building fences and pouring patios to carpentry and some electrical. Sometimes when the jobs were big enough, he even hired a few guys to work with him. By the time I was a teenager, he was semi-retired from the contracting work.

I didn't remember him ever mentioning college.

"You didn't save enough then…for college?"

He shook his head. "Oh no, I saved enough. Well, at least enough for the first two years. I figured that I would work while I was taking classes and keep saving and all that." He smiled and scratched his cheek. "What I didn't figure was that I'd meet your mother. Or that we'd fall in love. Or that I'd get her pregnant…and her just seventeen and still in school. And me, twenty-five."

"Pregnant?"

He nodded and then stood up and walked toward the kitchen.

"Dad?"

"I'm just getting a beer."

I scratched my fingernails along the stubble of my mustache, turning over the news. Did I have a brother or sister out there somewhere? Had they put their first child up for adoption?

Dad cracked the beer in the kitchen. He took a drink and then came back into the living room and lowered himself into his seat. He turned down the radio a little more.

"We got married about a month after the doctor gave your mother the news. I took the job with GM—Grandpa understood,

80

and it didn't really matter anyway 'cause the store went under within the next year—and I used my savings to put a down payment on a little house." He smiled, looking over my shoulder and out the window. "In our minds, we had a baby to get ready for."

"So no school then…no teaching?"

He shook his head. "At the time, I didn't really care. Her coming along into my life like she did…I knew that's what was supposed to happen."

I leaned back deeper into the couch and rubbed my forehead. "Something bad happened then? With the baby?"

He adjusted himself in his chair. His head nodded almost imperceptibly. "She lost the baby during birth." He shook his head and rubbed his eye with a finger. "We'd never really wanted that one. I mean, we weren't trying when we ended up pregnant is what I mean. But, after we lost him—well, like a year after we lost him—we started trying pretty hard. Two more miscarriages. Then nothing. Nothing for years. We wanted another one so bad, but it just didn't happen…well, not until you." He pointed at me. "And you were like that first one. I mean, not saying that we weren't happy as hell when you came along, but we weren't trying." He took in a breath and sighed. "I don't know how ready I was to be a dad anymore."

I leaned forward. "Is that why…I mean, why you were really pushing me to be a teacher?"

He took a drink of his beer. "Maybe." He shrugged. "And I think it's a good job, too. Good security. Summers off." He cleared his throat. "You weren't as shy near the end of high school. I could see you up in front of a classroom. You know, bright like you are."

I squeezed my hands over my knees. "I think switching majors was a mistake. I should have stayed with teaching."

He waved his hand toward me, a light-hearted swat. "Things work out," he said. "You find your way. I mean, I don't know if everything happens for a reason, but I think you end up doing what you're supposed to be doing. I got few regrets."

It was the most I'd ever heard him sound like my mother.

He scratched his eyebrow. "And, you're not going to be happy all the time no matter what you do. You can't. It's work. It's why they give you money to do it. Unhappiness is part of it. You just try not to let it win, you know?"

I nodded.

"Speaking of not winning," Dad said a moment later, turning up the radio, "I'm going to get ready for the Tigers."

81

We sat for awhile listening to the commentators. They were talking over the thing that the Tigers needed to start getting right. It was pretty obvious stuff. They needed to get their bats going. Their starters needed to keep from falling apart in the first inning. Their bullpen needed to back up the starters when they did pitch a decent five or six innings.

"No kidding?" Dad said to the radio. "They need to start hitting the ball?" He looked at me and shook his head. "Now why didn't Leyland think of that?" He pointed at the radio. "These guys here…they should really be doing the coaching. Geniuses."

I smiled.

Dad lay his head back into his chair. After awhile he closed his eyes again. The little fan turned back and forth. I waited until he was snoring before I left.

I was four blocks away, sweating under the heat of the overhead sun, when I looked at that red Pegasus bucking into flight on the side of the bar. I turned around and went back to the house, breaking into a jog about halfway.

"Dad?" I stood over him. "Wake up."

He opened his eyes. "What?"

"Come on. Get up. I'm taking you down to the Red Horse. We'll watch the game there."

"What are you—?"

"Just get up." I said, smiling.

As though he didn't have a choice, he got up, changed his shirt, and pushed a comb through his hair.

We were halfway down the driveway when he turned back for the house.

"Dad."

"Hold on just a second," he said, doing a half-jog toward the stoop. He popped up the steps and went inside. When he came out again, he had a Tigers cap on his head.

We spent the afternoon in front of a big-screen television. We ate popcorn and ordered a pitcher, and then another. Dad let me buy everything. Later, around the sixth inning, I got us a basket of wings and fries. Our fingers and lips shined with grease.

The beer had us feeling pretty good. We were cheering when the Tigers got some good hits. We were both standing up shouting when they won. The whole place was on its feet making noise.

"This was good," Dad said, as we walked home. "You going to go see those Roethke people tomorrow, then?" He said it with the th, so it rhymed with death-key.

I nodded. "I suppose I will."

The heat of the house and the beer was too much, and we both went to bed early. I looked out the window one last time into the dark backyard before getting into bed.

It was empty. No ember.

I don't think he smoked a cigarette the whole day.

10.

Abby Waters stepped out onto the white porch of the Roethke House, shielding her eyes from the sun. The police had taken the yellow tape down. A few extension ladders leaned against the gutters, and I could hear a tarp bucking around in the breeze. In the side yard, a dumpster sat half-filled with charred boards and shingles. Next door, two trucks were parked on the lawn of Carl Roethke's home. One of the trucks had the name of a local roofing company on the side. Men were sitting in the cabs, eating sandwiches.

I guessed by the streaks of gray in her hair that Abby was probably in her late fifties. I could never really tell after a certain age. She wore a long flower-print skirt, a black t-shirt, and an African-looking necklace. My forehead was dripping sweat, and I kept dabbing it with my sleeve. I only wanted to give her the envelope with the money in it. I hadn't planned to stay long, but she kept asking questions.

Turned out that she'd gone to U of M, too. She'd also had Professor Seager back in the day, and didn't I think he was wonderful. I told her I did. She asked about some of the bars, some of the bookstores. Many of them had closed. A few were still open under the same name. She asked me about a little Indian restaurant on Main St. It wasn't around anymore, and the news made her look not so much sad as tired. She nodded in a way that said, "Isn't that the way things always go."

When it seemed like she was running out of questions, she motioned behind her. "Denver, tell me, why do you care about this house?"

"What?"

She crossed her arms, but smiled slightly. "The house. Why do you care if it's here or not?"

Pushing my damp bangs from my forehead, I told her about high school and how I used to walk by the house some nights. "Even then I knew I wanted to write...or at least I thought so. I mean, it felt like I had something in me, something important I needed to do." I told her that back then I hadn't really read many of Roethke's poems. "Honestly, I still haven't, not a lot of them...mainly just the greenhouse poems. But still, he was from here. He grew up here. In Saginaw." I shook my head. "This brilliant poet was born here, went to school here..." I pointed at the house. "It's not like he has a statue or anything in town. It's just this house."

Abby nodded, smiling.

I dragged my sleeve across my dripping forehead. "And it's not just that he was famous, you know? It's that he was a poet...and what that means. When poets are good, they throw a light on what matters, you know?" I pointed her attention to the traffic flashing by on Gratiot, silhouettes in the driver's seats blurring past, staring straight ahead or talking on cell phones. "Everyone is going so fast all the time. Poets try to get us to look around, to live a little...to live better. Love the right things. Or at least be aware of the right things, right?" I shrugged. "I mean, that's big."

"Yes," she said.

I gestured at the house. "Clothes and tanning salons—the stuff that we think is important. None of that stuff is in poems, not good poems, anyway. Poems are about, I don't know. Root cellars, right? Going down into the dark and smelling the stinks and realizing that the dirt is breathing, that nothing—

Abby touched my arm. "He called it a 'congress of stinks'," she said. "Isn't that perfect?"

I nodded. "But, it's not just the word choices. It's the meaning. Going into that dark root cellar, finding the beauty even in it. But, you have to look, right? You have to probe the ordinary places...get beneath the surface to find the magic. I mean, it's even like that with people too sometimes, isn't it?" I thought of Ricky and Vance. "You have to get past their stinks to find that breathing person worth knowing."

She smiled and touched her fingers against her cheek. "I never really thought of it like—"

"I mean, if that's a question, why preserve this house? Then why preserve any historic building? Why preserve Henry Ford's home or even Greenfield Village? Why not just knock them all down? Why do we even have to ask the question? Is it just because Roethke was only a poet?" I raised my voice. "Only a poet?!"

Abby was smiling, nodding. "Exactly," she said. "What you're saying, it sounds like something he would have said." She told me that Roethke often said that poets aren't more indispensible than engineers or scientists, but they are no less so, either.

I nodded. "What did that one poet write...:

85

It is difficult
to get the news from poems
yet men die miserably every day
for lack
of what is found there."

Abby looked at me and smiled. "That's William Carlos Williams," she said.

We stood for a moment on the porch of the Roethke House with Williams' words still resonating in the air around us. She looked happy but, staring out at the steady flow of traffic, her joy slowly faded, like gravity was really working against her smile.

"Let's go in," she said, fanning her hand at her face. "It's so hot out here."

While she opened the door, I slipped the envelope from my back pocket. Once inside, I took a few steps toward the piano that I'd seen through the window earlier that summer.

"That's the actual piano he practiced on as a boy," she said, raising her voice above the dehumidifiers scattered throughout the ground floor rooms.

I touched my fingers along the smooth fall.

"Did you have piano lessons ever?" she asked, watching me.

I shook my head.

"All three of my boys did. Getting them to practice was so difficult that I eventually quit with the lessons. Theodore, though, he practiced for hours every day by choice. Poetry, piano, tennis…it was like if he wanted to be good at something he was, through sheer determination." She tapped a finger into the open palm of her other hand. "I don't think the poems ever came easy for him, either. It's cliché, I know, but it's like he went through labor for them. And, yet, he seldom felt that they were good enough. Isn't that sad? A man of that caliber not having it in him to admire his own work."

"It is sad."

She motioned for me to follow her through the foyer and into the next room where there was a fireplace and a dining room set. Pulling out a chair, she sat down at the table. "See how the fireplace is set at an angle? It's the same over in Carl's house," she said, gesturing out the window.

I leaned down and looked across at the fieldstone.

"A local historian thinks they might be Sears and Roebuck homes," she said. She pointed out the window at the other house. "I

86

don't like to go in there, though. We found a decaying raccoon carcass in the living room the last time we went in."

I pulled out a chair and sat at the table. I counted four dehumidifiers.

"They've cleaned up much of the mess," Abby said, talking over the drone, "but they're still trying to pull as much moisture as they can from the walls."

I nodded, pushing the envelope across the table to her. I'd added a hundred dollars of my own money. "It's not much," I said.

"What?"

I pointed at the envelope. "It's not a lot of money."

She waved her hand. "Oh, let's just go into the kitchen," she said. "I can hardly hear out here."

I followed her across the old wooden floors and past the staircase that lead to the darkness of the second level. She closed the door to the kitchen, dampening the noise from the other rooms down to a murmur. I looked around at the paint peeling in large patches from the ceiling and walls.

"We won't repaint until after a historical paint analysis," Abby said. "We eventually want to recreate the rooms as close to as they were when he lived here."

She walked into the middle of the floor and spread out her arms. "I remember seeing it for the first time. This room," she said. "It was so small. I thought, 'Now how could they have danced in here?' Otto was a big man, after all."

I could almost see them spinning. Otto, tipsy on whiskey. Little Theodore hanging on. His mother watching them, watching the pans sliding from the shelves. "My Papa's Waltz," I said just above a whisper.

Abby smiled and nodded. "This is that kitchen. You know, if you open all the doors, each room leads into the other. Maybe the dance started in the kitchen and then spun around the first floor and back to the kitchen." She took a step and spun a half circle herself. Her skirt twirled around her legs. "It's like standing in the middle of a poem, isn't it?" She looked at me. "You know, some people read that as a violent poem. The frowning mother, the scraped knuckle, beating time on the boy's head—they say it's symbolic of the father's abusiveness."

Shaking my head, I recalled a professor at Michigan I'd had that pushed for that kind of reading. He said that a lot of Roethke's personal writing suggested that he feared his father and even hated him. "Something had to be behind that hate," the professor had said, leaning dramatically with both hands on the podium.

I didn't buy it. I always saw it as Roethke remembering a rare moment with Otto—a moment when a little drinking loosened him up and allowed him to be carefree. Roethke's father was a hard-working man, probably a workaholic. That scraped knuckle had nothing to do with child abuse. It was just from being married to work, like my dad's own work-worn hands.

For one brief moment in one brief night, Otto forgot about his palms "caked hard by dirt." He stumbled into dancing and lost his responsibilities. He forgot the needs of all those flowers out there in the darkness of the greenhouses. Forgot about regulating the heat of the boilers. Forgot the manure. He was just a father with a son, dancing blissfully in a whiskey-induced epiphany of being alive. If the mother was frowning, it was only because she was worried about what might be broken. No wonder Roethke hung on like death, clinging to his father's shirt. He felt the moment fleeting. He was being twirled off to bed, to sleep. He knew that it would end, and Otto would wake with the talk of the greenhouses and the carnations in his mouth, like always. He would be distant again and fixated on the flowers.

I thought of my father and me walking home from the Red Horse the night before. A little tipsy himself, he slapped me on the back and said that he was proud of me. The stars. The fireflies. My dad and I feeling good from beer that I'd bought for us. It was a moment that I wouldn't have minded clinging to for awhile myself.

Abby dropped into a chair by the door.

I shook my head. "I don't see how anybody can see that as a dark poem."

She said nothing in reply. When I looked over at her, she was crying.

I swallowed.

She took off her glasses and massaged her fingertips through her eyes. "I'm sorry," she said. "I didn't bring you in here for this."

I took a step toward her. "Are you okay?"

"It's just—all of it, everything—it's just been a horrible time." She told me that two weeks before, the city had sent an inspector through the house as a precaution after the fire. He checked all the knob and tube wiring. Even though the insurance inspector provided proof that the fire was caused by rodents chewing the wires, the city inspector felt otherwise. "He said the whole house would have to be rewired," she said. She held her hand over her mouth and sighed into it. "The lowest estimate we've had so far has been twenty thousand."

I shook my head and leaned against the stove. "What would the deductible be for that?"

She laughed bitterly. "Insurance covers none of it, not for rewiring."

I thought of the money in the envelope I'd given her. It was peanuts. "Twenty thousand dollars?" I asked.

"At least," she said. She brushed at her cheeks. "We have nothing. When our board voted to buy the house, the vote passed by a thin margin. The whole thing was a losing proposition, but to keep it from being closed to the public, we knew we had to buy it. We're paying for it out of our own pockets...the mortgage, the utilities, the operating costs." She took a long breath. "Now with these new expenses—well, most of the board wants out. They say we don't need to own the house to celebrate the man's legacy. As one board member said, 'The man wrote the poems. The house didn't do anything.'" She sighed. "I sometimes wonder if he isn't right. I don't know. It's just that a city like this...it needs this house."

I touched one of the cold burners on the stovetop. "So what does all of this mean?"

She sighed. "If we can keep the house, the city will condemn it until the repairs are made," she said. "We would go on making mortgage payments, but lose any of the meager revenue that comes with having presentations and workshops here." She said that it might go on for years, a decade even. "With the board we have now, that's not going to happen. My guess is that at next month's board meeting, they are going to vote to sell."

"To who?"

She hugged her arms across her chest. "To whomever wants to buy it." She wagged her finger at the air in front of her. "And there are buyers. There's a man in Bay City who wants the house for a private residence." She laughed hollowly. "Then there's a landlord right here in Saginaw who wants to break the place up into two apartments—"

"What?"

She coughed out another exasperated little laugh. "I know, I know, but it's true. A landlord was renting out Carl's house for years before we were finally able to buy it. The tenants were horrible to the interior over there."

She rubbed her palms together. "If it goes up on the market, it won't stay there for long. The man in Bay City comes from old money...probably never worked a day in his life. He's a huge poetry enthusiast. We asked him for donations on any number of occasions.

Has he ever once given so much as a penny?" She shook her head and then answered her own question. "Not once. He clearly wants us to fail." She looked at the floor. "I suspect that some of our newest board members might even be friends of his. Anyway, looks like he's going to win. Or, at the very least, we're going to lose."

A car honked out on Gratiot. I thought of the roofers outside. "How long did it take you to raise the two thousand for the deductible after the fire?"

Abby laughed. "We were lucky to raise three hundred dollars." She said that she had to sell a car that she'd inherited when her father died. "It wasn't an antique or anything, just an extra car. I probably needed to sell it, anyway."

Someone came in the front door, big footsteps stomping across the floor. A moment later, the door to the kitchen opened, and a man walked in behind Abby. She flinched, then started wiping her eyes.

"Sorry. Didn't mean to scare you." His tanned face and arms looked like stained wood. He wore a dirty t-shirt and jeans ground in with black patches of what looked like tar. "Just going to fill this up," he said, holding a water bottle out for us to see. He turned on the tap. "Don't let me interrupt."

"We were just stepping out," Abby said. She stood.

The man looked back over his shoulder as his bottle filled. "We should have all the new decking down by the end of the day," he said, smiling.

Abby turned to him and nodded. "Well, I don't want you and your crew up there if it gets too hot. If it doesn't feel right, just take the day off and come back tomorrow."

He smiled. "Well, ma'am, if we let the heat keep us from working, you wouldn't have a roof on this place until October. Always hot on a roof."

Something about his bulky forearms reminded me of Vance.

"Anyway," he said, "gotta figure you'll lose a guy or two to heatstroke on every job." He turned off the water and started spinning the cap back on his bottle. "Bury 'em where they fall is what we say." He leaned back against the sink.

Abby looked at him

His serious face cracked into smiling.

"Oh," she said, waving her hand at him. Shaking her head, she turned toward the door.

I followed her back out to the porch. I could taste the heat in the breaths I took.

"It's oppressive out here," she said.

I wasn't sure what to do. I started for the steps. Other men were talking up on the roof. They had a radio with them pushing out classic rock. Sounded like The Who...Roger Daltrey singing something about love falling from the trees.

I turned toward Abby. "So what's your plan?"

She smoothed a pinched thumb and finger along the closed flap of my envelope. "No plan. There's nothing to be done. The board has been unequivocal in its opinion about selling the place. I'm throwing in the proverbial towel." She looked up at me with watery eyes. "You get older, Denver. The fight goes out of you. The idea of not wringing people's necks every day to get them to care becomes appealing." She looked out at the traffic absently. "I was at a dinner party with friends last night, people I used to count among the hopeful. They had nothing but venom for this town. Everyone seems to be giving up." She crossed her arms. "Maybe with the extra time, I'll start to write again." Looking up into the porch ceiling, she wondered aloud if maybe all of this wasn't meant to happen. "It may just be time for me to move on and cut this albatross free."

I started down the stairs. I didn't feel like there was anything I could do. "I wonder what Roethke would say about all of this," I said.

"I have no idea," she said. "He'd probably find it all very predictable. His big suspicion was that most people didn't care about poetry."

I started across the lawn, not really sure how to say goodbye, and not really sure, in so many ways, where I was going.

Nearing the sidewalk, I stopped and turned around. "What about the greenhouses? Could I see them?"

Abby shook her head, fanning herself with her hand. She looked at me as though I were a child or a simpleton. "They were torn down," she said, "a long time ago."

"Oh," I said. "Okay." I turned to walk away.

Above the noise of Gratiot's traffic, she called out to me. "And just so you know, his last name is pronounced 'Ret-Key.'"

11.

It was going to turn out to be a strange night, maybe the night that accounted for everything else. I walked for a long time after I left the Roethke House, picturing it busted up into apartments, a gutted shell. Tenants moving in and moving out with no sense of what it had been. Tenants eroding the place. The day's heat made my thoughts angrier.

There was that sonuvabitch from Bay City that just wanted the house for himself. There'd be no more tours, no more community writing workshops, no more Roethke birthday celebrations or Roethke scholars coming in to give talks in what was once Roethke's living room. No more standing in the kitchen of "My Papa's Waltz."

I could tell, too, that Abby was done. The fight was out of her. Too many years of disappointment.

When I got there, I walked around Old Town for awhile. The Red Eye coffee shop was full of people. There was music, the murmur of conversations. Some high school kids were outside leaning up against the wall, smoking. I bummed a cigarette and a light from one guy with long dreadlocks, but only took a few drags before I flicked it into the street.

Smoking. It reminded me too much of Heather.

"Hey, what the fuck, man?"

I looked back. The kid who'd fronted me the cigarette looked at me and then out toward the street where I'd tossed the butt.

I shrugged my shoulders.

He flipped me the bird. "You suck, dude."

I walked past a tattoo place, turned on to Hancock, and then walked past the furniture store and into Fralia's for a sandwich. For awhile I walked around taking small bites from a Reuben, not really tasting it. I ended up outside of Bruce's coffee shop. A poster in the window featured a picture of Joshua sitting on a stool with his guitar and singing into the mic. I could tell that he was having a good time. They were advertising live music Thursday, Friday, and Saturday nights.

Joshua was moving up. Good for him. He was a nice enough guy.

The door opened, and Bruce walked out. He was in his requisite polo and khakis. "I thought that was you, Denver."

I had a mouthful of corn beef, Swiss cheese, and sauerkraut. Chewing, I nodded to him, lowering my sweating brow into my sleeve.

"Fucking hot," I mumbled.

He walked up. "I'm glad I ran into you. You never picked up your amplifier and microphone."

Amplifier and microphone? I never saw myself needing them again. I shrugged and started to walk away. "Keep 'em," I said, talking around the food in my mouth like Ricky would have done.

He pulled me to an abrupt stop by my sleeve. "I don't want them. Joshua has his own equipment now."

Swallowing, I looked at his hand on my sleeve. "I'll come by sometime and get them then."

"But I want you to take them now."

I jerked my sleeve out of his grip. "I don't have a car."

"That's not my problem."

What the hell was it with this guy? Turning from him, I shook my head. "You know what, just kiss my ass, Bruce. I can't do it today."

He talked to my back. "I'll just throw them away, then. I'll just put them to the street."

I turned and walked straight toward him, driving him back a couple steps. His face paled. "Then do it. Throw it away. I really don't give a shit."

He held up his hands. "Okay. Okay. Just get them when you can. Within the next few days or something," he said, walking back to the coffee shop's entrance.

Heart still pounding, I tossed the second half of my sandwich into a dumpster in an alley. I leaned against the stained brick wall. Not far from my feet were scattered the bones of some small animal. Mopping sweat from my forehead, I kept thinking of Bruce's face, the fear I'd put in it. He had looked like he believed that I might actually do something. Something physical. I don't know that anyone had ever looked at me that way. I liked it, and I didn't like it.

With the heat of the day on my skin and the salty corn beef dehydrating my mouth, I needed something to drink. I ended up at the Hamilton Street Pub. After a beer and some air conditioning, the bartender let me use the phone to call Heywood.

"I'm just chillin' tonight," he said.

"Yeah, but, I don't get many nights off, man."

He sighed. "Hold on."

Hand over the mouthpiece, he talked to someone on his end. Then he came back on. "I'll be there."

I'd had three beers by the time he arrived.

Heywood stirred his straw through a second rum and coke. "What happened to Portland?"

I picked a half-popped kernel out of the popcorn basket and turned it in my fingers, studying it. "I don't know. Didn't feel right." I dropped the kernel back in with the others. "Nothing feels exactly right, you know?"

He took a drink and then set his glass back into its wet spot on the table. "You writing?"

I shook my head. "Not a word." I took a long drink from my beer, feeling it tingle in my cheeks.

A few college-aged girls walked in and up to the bar. I turned my head and watched them. It was a night for shorts and skirts—legs. Heather had great legs.

"Who me? Am I writing? Damn nice of you to ask."

"What?" I shook my head a few times and looked at him. "I'm sorry, man. Have you been doing some writing?"

He nodded. "I'm working on three diff—"

"What if you didn't have the urge?"

"What?"

"The urge to write…to create." I took another drink and banged the empty bottle down on the table. "It'd be so much easier, wouldn't it?"

"What'd be easier?"

I chopped my hand through the air in front of me. "All of it. Just not worrying about working on a poem or rewriting or coming up with…I don't know, any of it. Be easier just to be a little more normal." My hands started flipping around in front of me. "The whole creating thing. Getting mad at yourself because you're not working on something. I just imagine being like my dad, you know? Change out some rotted posts on the split-rail fence. Just sitting in his chair, listening to the Tigers, sipping a beer, and looking out the window now and again at the new posts in his fence. That's all the man needs to feel good. It'd be so much better to just work and watch television and fish or golf or…I don't know." I set my hands on the table. "I'd like to be like the people who say, 'You write poetry? Why?' You know, like it's a waste of time. I mean, I wish that's how I felt. In fact, I do feel that way, but I can't shake the need. I hate it, feeling like I'm failing all the time. Ever since I started really writing, that's how I feel."

94

Heywood adjusted his glasses. "Don't know anyone's got it easy."

I nodded slowly. "I know. You're right. Still, I think there'd be something to being just a guy, you know? A guy. I'd like to be a guy whose back hurts, and he figures out that it hurts because of his old mattress. He's been pretty good with his money, so he can afford a new mattress. So he buys one. Then he sleeps on it, and in the morning his back feels better. He's really proud of himself about being good with his money. And his back feels good, you know? And then that's it. He doesn't feel like he has to write a fucking poem about his new mattress. He doesn't lose sleep because the mattress poem he's working on lacks imagery. He just climbs into bed and sleeps well. That's it."

Heywood laughed. "Mattress poem." He shook his head. "You buggin'."

"Maybe I am," I said, standing up. The room sloped a little bit to the left and then righted itself.

"You good?"

"Yeah. I'm just going to get another beer." I walked over to the bar, ordered another, and brought it back to the table.

"Well," Heywood said, "I think it's cool that you sticking around for awhile, anyway."

I shrugged. "I don't know for how long, but I'm not going anywhere just yet." I took a long drink. "I don't think, though, that I can stay here much longer. Everything here—in Saginaw—it kind of turns to shit, you know?"

I thought I saw him roll his eyes. He picked up his drink and finished it down to the last slivers of ice. "I think I'm gonna bail, D. I told my girl I'd only be out for a couple of hours."

"Has it been two hours?"

"Been long enough."

I pounded half the beer. "Wait up. I'll walk out with you."

Standing, he nodded. "Aight."

It was dark. Everything was still sticky and hot, like a fever. There were voices in Old Town. Young people shifted in and out of bars and coffee shops, pretending they lived in a big city until they could actually move to one. This wasn't a place for young people. If they stayed, they got old too fast.

A group of girls came up to us. One set her hands on my chest and looked up into my face. She was skinny and plain, but had pretty green eyes. "Don't leave," she said, nodding toward the entrance of the pub. "It's early. Anything could happen."

Her friends pulled her away. "Never mind her," one of them called back to me. "She just turned twenty-one." They disappeared into the pub.

For some time after, I could feel the places where her hands had been on me.

Heywood lit a Black and Mild. He was parked close to the river. A fishy smell wafted up on the air from it. We walked a few blocks to get to his car, but didn't talk. I could tell that he'd had enough of me. Whatever the beer had been doing for my mood, which wasn't much, was gone.

He leaned against his driver side door. The little cigar flared orange, dimly lighting his bored face.

White boy from the township. His girlfriend was right all along. Waste of time.

I paced in the road. "Look, man, I'm sorry I'm not good company." Across the river in the distance, a pair of headlights drifted slowly around Ojibway Island Drive. "I'm just in a funk."

He exhaled a cloud that drifted up and dissipated in the darkness. "It's cool. Been a funky summer for you." He dropped the cigar and tiptoed it out. He smiled. "You want to get blunted?"

I walked around to the passenger door and pulled up on the locked handle.

"Guess you do," he said over the roof of the car. He got in and unlocked my door.

Heywood handed me the blunt first. I sparked it and took a long drag and held it. It was like taking in helium. Not the squeaky voice, just the idea that something was in me, buoying me. I waited to float up off the seat. It felt like it might just happen.

The streets were crawling with pedestrians, passing in and out of streetlights, shadows crossing streets and going into bars. Fucking ghosts.

"Release it, Dawg. That herb is ill." He took the blunt from my fingers and laughed. "You gonna be a zombie."

I exhaled and dropped my smiling skull back against the seat. Heywood's tight-lipped inhaling filled the car. I laughed. "It's weird, you know, but I'm going to miss that job when it's over."

He was holding his smoke. He purred a sound of "I'm listening" in his throat.

"It was simple, you know. Like, Thoreau-simple."

He exhaled a cloud against the windshield, laughing. "What?"

"Nothing. It's just that it wasn't a bad routine. I liked walking around the place and seeing some damn wall that I'd painted and thinking, 'That wall looks good because of me.' I mean, I could actually see some difference that I'd made. Then I'd go home, eat, listen to a little baseball, and fall asleep. Usually I was too tired to worry about anything, even poems." I took the blunt. "I'm almost jealous of that...people who get to live that way." I took another hit and could feel an aura around my fingers.

Heywood looked up the street. "Lots of rollers in Old Town tonight."

"Hmm?" I asked, holding smoke.

"Five-O."

"Hmm?"

He looked at me. "Police, man."

Nodding, I exhaled and then touched my fingers over my cheeks. "My whole face feels shot through with novacaine."

"Give me that," he said, taking the blunt from my fingers. "Off the chain weed like this is wasted on you." He took a hit, held it, and then released. He looked at me and shook his head. "Look at you," he said, smiling, "all lifted." Then, after a moment, he shook his head again. "That shit you're selling about people not worrying about things. Living simple, having it good? You're wack, man. People may not be worrying about writing poems, but they're worrying. You know what they're worrying about?" He looked at me.

I shook my head, feeling my brain drifting back and forth.

"They worrying about money. Everything is money for most people. Like my mama. That's all she thinks about. Is she making enough? How can she make more? What store's having sales?" He shook his head. "And, when she has something new, she don't tell you how much she likes it." He pointed at me. "She tell you how much that shit cost. If she could get it at a good price, she'd wear a dress made of spider webs, just so she could tell people, 'What? This? This ol' spider web dress? Well this was only nine dollars.' She'd be twirling around. All kinds of bugs sticking to her...she wouldn't care."

I started laughing.

"Shit's true. That's how most people do. Money. It eats them up. You don't have it bad because you worry about writing poems all the time. Shit, you got it good. That's something real at least. You're not worrying about a better car or new jeans or..."

Heywood leaned and looked out his window. Another cop car went through the cross street two blocks away. He licked his fingers, pulled the cherry off the blunt, and sprinkled it in the ashtray. "Don't ever say you want to be like everyone else," he said, touching

97

his finger to the end of the blunt and checking it for heat, before dropping it in his pocket. "Everyone is miserable, like Mama says. If you like things—things that money can buy—then you always unhappy because you know that what you got isn't as good as what others got. It's never enough."

My voice sounded like someone else was talking in the car. "It's hard, though, you know?"

"No shit, it's hard." He punched me in the arm. "Always hard…that's all part of it. If it was easy, we'd all go the same way."

Something about that moment. It made me think of the softly ringing bells of levy's winter pony.

I listened for them. I didn't hear anything.

Heywood looked out the window again. "I'm ghost. Too many people down here having a good time," he said. "Police are everywhere." He looked at me. "You need a ride?"

I didn't want one. I wanted to walk home and clear my head. I was no farther along than I'd been when I'd first moved back. No girlfriend. No job. No poems. No prospects. I shook my head. "I'm going to walk, think a little bit."

He took my hand and pulled me into a hug. "Be easy, brother." He looked at me after the hug and laughed, shaking his head. "You gonna be all right?"

I nodded and told him that I'd talk to him soon.

Getting out, I closed the door. I could hear the voices of people out on the streets. People laughing, yelling. Up overhead the full moon reflected a melted image of itself on the Saginaw River. I knocked on the passenger window.

Heywood leaned across the seat and rolled it down. "What?"

"Stay here a second. I gotta take a leak."

He laughed. "Hurry up," he said. He rolled up the window.

I leaned against the back door, closed my eyes, and emptied my head. I started to pee. When I finished, I tapped the roof. Heywood's car grumbled away down Niagara. I watched his taillights until he turned left onto Madison and disappeared.

Walking in the other direction, I knew that Court Street was the best way home.

A noise behind me was coming up fast. Before I could turn around, someone on a skateboard shot past on my left. I stopped walking and held my hand over my heart. Fucker, I thought. He kept going, right leg stepping down now and again, giving him speed.

"I wish I skateboarded," I said, walking again. "I do," I said, as though someone had challenged me.

Headlights were coming over the Court Street Bridge. I shielded my eyes. I couldn't stop smiling. "I'm still really high," I mumbled. I heard myself say it and I laughed because I'd only meant to think it. There were people walking around. A guy with long hair was sitting on the ground with his back against a brick wall. He was cross-legged and playing a guitar. A pretty girl in a flower print summer dress was sitting next to him watching his fingers. Her blonde hair was crazy pretty curtained over her shoulders. I stopped and listened. It wasn't a song I recognized. He was singing something about the next time she saw him he wouldn't be the him she once knew. He'd be hard-hearted and cold.

"Did you write that?"

He looked up at me. His bangs fell over his face, and he flipped them back. "Writing it now," he said. "Not done yet."

I gave him a double thumbs-up. "Keep going. Sounding good."

The girl looked up at me and smiled. She looked down and then up again. "Your fly's down, dude."

"Oh, shit. Sorry." I zipped up and started walking again. "Thanks," I called back. They were laughing behind me. I didn't care.

I went past the entrance to what was once the Court Street Gallery. Back in high school I'd gone to some poetry readings there hosted by this sultry-voiced, tattooed chick. As far as I knew, she was gone. I stood back and looked up into the darkened windows. The Court Street Gallery was gone, too.

Everything good in this place dies or goes somewhere else, I thought.

I thought of the Roethke House. It was slipping away, too.

A car slowed behind me and then honked. I jumped.

"Get the fuck out the road, white."

I stepped back up on the sidewalk and kept going. I got the walk light on Michigan and ran across. There weren't people on the sidewalk anymore. I tried to imagine how long I had to go before I got home. It felt like days. I couldn't stop yawning. I called myself a dumbass for not accepting the ride from Heywood. That was my life…too much looking back and seeing what I should have done, what I should have said.

Or shouldn't have.

Out of nowhere, I was hungry. Hungrier than I'd ever been. I thought about the chips a gas station might have or the burger and fries of some fast food place. The insides of my cheeks seeped with saliva.

I kept walking. Goddamn, I was hungry. It was more than hunger. It was like I was hollowed out, like I could eat forever if I ever found anything. That was, of course, if I didn't curl up under a bush and fall asleep first. I was as tired as I was hungry. I closed my eyes, trying to nap while I walked.

I passed a Lutheran church on the right side of the road. Half a block later, I passed a Presbyterian church on the left side. If either would have had a soup kitchen, I would have eaten. If they'd had a shelter, I would have slept.

Both were dark and looked locked up for the night.

On the next block, a bank. I didn't need money. I looked up and down the cross streets for a light, a sign—a restaurant, a gas station, a convenience store. I swallowed a mouthful of spit.

There was nothing.

Then, voices. People yelling. Laughing. How many blocks had I walked since Michigan? I didn't know. I was sure I'd never get home. Never eat. Never sleep.

Then there was a sound distinct from the rest. I knew it immediately. A child was crying. The street sign above. Bond Street.

The kid was on the sidewalk—a tiny silhouette in the darkness—maybe three or four years old. Streetlight glowed down on me. I stood watching him, listening. It wasn't whimpering or sniveling. It was sobbing, the noises of loss, abandonment.

There was so little light on his street—a couple dim porch lights, but mainly just the gray-black of the night's available light. Everything was silhouettes.

I don't know how much time passed as I watched him and listened. I kept waiting. Surely an adult shadow would come out of one of the houses and gather him up into its arms.

It came to me after a minute. If someone was going to comfort this child, it had to be me. There was nobody else. I was the only one.

The little shadow waddled out into the street, yelled some word I couldn't understand, and then went back to the sidewalk. The voice made me think that he was a boy.

"Are you okay?" I called from twenty feet away, trying not to startle him.

His little head snapped toward me, and he stopped crying.

"Where's your house? Are you lost?" I took a few steps his way.

He studied me a moment longer before turning and bolting down the sidewalk.

Fuck.

"Hey? Wait. Don't run. I'm not going to hurt you." I shook my head, wondering if I'd chased him away from his front yard.

I started after him, stopping briefly where I'd seen him crying. The house was dark. A couch on the porch. The others were dark, too, or flickering faintly with television light. A few air conditioners hummed along with droning window fans.

I looked. The kid was at the end of the block, crossing the street.

I jogged, trying to keep up with his distancing silhouette. Little or not, he was fast.

"I'm not going to hurt you," I shouted. I had no wind.

A dog threw itself at a chain link fence, barking at me. My heart jumped up into my throat.

Jolted with adenaline, I ran faster and started to gain on the kid.

I started across another street after him. Headlights washed over me. The driver slammed the brakes, the sound like some giant bird dying. I held up my hands toward the grill of an SUV that was only feet from me.

"You stupid motherfucker!"

I shouted an apology and ran the rest of the way across the street.

"Hey!"

In the passenger seat, the outline of a head like a storm cloud. His hand held up the shadow of a gun for me to see.

"Got a death wish, you punk bitch?"

I couldn't move. I tried to apologize again and to tell him about this little kid. This lost little kid. This child.

No words came out.

A porch flashed into light across the street. Then another. The driver gunned the gas, and the SUV squealed away.

When I turned around, heart still racing, the kid was gone. Everything was black and hot and quiet. Sirens wailed somewhere in the city. I'd almost been killed, twice. Shit. The kid could fend for himself.

Then something moved in the darkness of the park on my right. The skeletal outline of a jungle gym was like a modern sculpture in the distance. A bench, too…and someone sitting on it. I started toward it, staggering with everything that had just happened.

"Is that you, kid?" I took a few more steps. "Kid?"

"No, it ain't." An adult shadow stood up from the bench. Then two more walked out from under a pine tree.

Something shot up my spine. I took a step back. "Okay," I said. "Sorry."

"Hold up a minute, chief."

One of the shadows stepped toward me. "Yeah, let's talk."

I turned around and started back down Bond toward Court Street. My heart was sore with pounding. Holy shit, I thought. This is stupid. So goddamn stupid.

Giant shadows of trees hunched over the dark street. I didn't look back. The light of Court seemed as though it were at the end of a tunnel.

I imagined footsteps behind me.

Exploding into barking, the dog slammed into the fence again when I passed. "Jesus Christ," I said, catching my stolen breath. It followed me along the chain-link, growling and sometimes barking. Its teeth flashed in the dim light. A door opened and someone shouted for the animal to shut the hell up.

I listened for footsteps. I walked, half-jogging. Court Street was ahead, cars passing back and forth, a police car briefly among them. I almost called out for it.

The dog started barking again.

Court Street. All that perfect street light. That activity. Safety.

12.

It was dark. I opened my eyes to the blurred, dizzying world. Blinking, I slowly made what turned out to be a house across the street come into focus. Its front window wavered with pale television light. Cool grass prickled against my cheek. I was on somebody's lawn. After a few seconds, the house across the street went out of focus again. I lay for a time waiting for it to return. My ears were ringing.

When I finally lifted my face, a dull pain on the back of my head began to throb. I felt over the lump and winced. It was as though somebody had wedged half a golf ball under the skin, a knot of flesh simmering beneath my fingers. I rolled on my side, and something slid from my back.

I felt around in the grass. My wallet. I sat for a moment with it in my hand, feeling the pulsing pain in the back of my head like someone tapping with a small hammer. The house across the street was blurry. I looked at it, blinking, trying to bring it back into focus. Things started coming to me. The little kid. Almost being hit by the SUV. The men in the park. The dog.

It was still barking.

"I'm not going to tell you to shut up again," someone hollered, followed by the sound of a slap. The animal yelped and then whimpered into quiet.

I tried to stand. A sensation gathered tingling in the back of my throat, and I dropped to my knees and vomited up the Reuben and beer. I stayed on all fours spitting, waiting to vomit again. After a minute, I felt a little better. Steadying my back against a tree, I inched up to standing again.

I walked out to the light of Court and stood under a street lamp. I opened my wallet. The money was gone. Everything else looked to still be there. My expired license, my student I.D., my emergency calling card with no minutes left on it.

My feet started for home. Walking, I didn't feel nauseous anymore. My vision was better. The only thing I had to remind me that I'd been knocked out and robbed was my empty wallet, the lump on the back of my skull, and a dull headache.

103

I must have gone six or seven blocks before I realized something else was missing. Those bastards. They'd taken the Fordite ring that my mom and dad had given me. The joint on my finger was sore and the skin was scraped from someone yanking on the ring to remove it. I imagined my unconscious body on some stranger's lawn and these men going over me for anything of value.

Fuck this place, I thought. It became the rhythm that moved my feet. Fuck. This. Place. Fuck. This. Place. What kind of town was it? You try to help a lost little kid in the night. What do you get as reward? Threatened with a gun. Knocked out and robbed. Ransacked.

I had to go somewhere. Portland, Oregon. Portland, Maine. I didn't care. Fueled with bitterness—replaying things in my head—I put blocks behind. Amidst the headlights and taillights, I made it to Davenport and turned left. Davenport became State. It didn't seem like it was very long before I was at the Red Horse and turning down the street to my father's house.

When I let myself in, I looked with relief at his empty chair. I had nothing in me for questions. I went into the kitchen and checked the green numbers on the microwave. One in the morning. In the light, I examined my fingertips after touching the lump on the back of my head. No blood as far as I could tell. I paced around, deciding whether or not I should go to bed, remembering something about it being a bad idea to sleep after being knocked unconscious. Still, I was so tired.

I went past the counter again and noticed a yellow package with my name on it. I looked at the return address.

Heather.

Something icy shot through my intestines. I turned the package over in my hands, feeling the glossy packing tape along the edges. It felt like she'd sent me a book…probably something like *Poetry for Dummies* or *Dealing with Your Depression*. I started for the stairs. I didn't want Dad to come down and find me in the kitchen. I wasn't up to explaining anything to him or having him spot the missing ring.

Up in my room, I opened the package with a penknife. Inside was an issue of the *Kenyon Review*. I knew immediately that she had a poem in it. Holy shit. The *Kenyon* fucking *Review*! What I couldn't quite wrap my mind around was why she'd sent it to me. How many contributor copies could they have given to her that she would waste one on me? Was she that petty that she needed to send me yet another of her writing victories?

The rhythm of my father's snoring came through the wall.

I set the magazine on my desk, unable to bring myself to look at the table of contents. I didn't want to see her name, even though I knew it was there. I almost tossed the packaging into the garbage before realizing that she'd included a letter. I pulled it out and unfolded it. I held the paper to my nose and smelled her scent of cigarettes and perfume. Touching my fingers over the back of my head, feelings the contours of the lump, I read:

Dear Denver,

It must seem strange to you to get a package from me, especially after our last conversation. I send this to you only because I think I must give credit where credit is due. When I started writing more experimental poems, you were quite outspoken in your opposition. You attacked experimentation as a fad. You said it's what poets who have nothing to say do when they want it to look like they have something to say. You said professors teach experimentation because they can't really teach their students to have something to say. You called my poems derivative. If I attacked your poems in kind, it was only because you backed me into a defensive position.

I felt like I hated you.

What you ended up doing, though, was pushing me. I scrutinized every one of my poems through your eyes. I threw many away. I heard your voice asking, "But how does the experiment serve the message? Are you doing what you're doing to get published, or are you doing it because this new way is the only way that the poem can be said…the way it has to be said?"

You didn't make me stop writing experimentally. You made me write better. You made me experiment with a purpose. I realized when I received an acceptance from the *Kenyon Review* that it had as much to do with you as it had to do with me. For that, I thank you.

When you have the time or the inclination, look at page 62.

I hope you are doing well in Saginaw. I hope you are doing something worthwhile with your rebel soul. I admire you more than you probably know or would guess.

Love,

Heather

With shallow breaths, I read the letter several times, guessing each time that there was something I was mis-reading. Then I picked up the magazine and turned to the page she'd indicated.

I read:

Heather Stevenson
God Is In What Is Not Made
—for Denver

"The cosmos may be found; but the ideas we form about it, and the things we say about it, are made." -Walter Truett Anderson from the *Introduction to The Truth About Truth*

Ah, a cryptic quote, the perfect way to make your poem seem important.

This Tomato

tomato, made
knife, made

my hand
also made
by a mother

mother is found
and made

Oh, for God's sake. I pushed her to this? Why was she blaming me?

this tomato
in my hand
which was made
by a mother
but also found
on the breast
of the mother

and this knife
with which
I make the cut

I Made This Sandwich

this tomato sandwich
is just made

this tomato sandwich is not God

but the movement it took to make
and the pleasure it gives

the pleasure the sandwich gives is God

the incision the knife made
the clean cut through the skin
of the tomato
not the cut itself
not the slices
but the movement that made the cut

God was that movement

Then something dawned on me. I knew this poem. It was
the poem I'd told her she needed to write. It was the poem about
making her mom tomato sandwiches...

Once The Hand That Cut

lay on the mother's breast
and the breath of the mother
also moved through me

the breath was found
not made

but the breast, made
the milk of the breast, made
abundantly

the milk of the breast was not God
the nurturing, God

God Is Not

in this poem – is not
in the words
I am writing
in this poem
or this pen
or even in my fingers
that grip the pen
that is in my hand
as I am writing
this poem
where God is not

But What Is Moving

my hand, my fingers
this pen

what is moving
from my mind
where God also is not
to my fingers
to this pen

but not the what
the moving itself
there is no what
God is not a what

God is not in the movement

God Is The Movement

but God is also not
in the words of this poem

so the poem itself
does not matter

The Poem Is The Mark

where God happened
where God was
but the poem is not God

God Stays In My Breathing

in the pulse
the life moving
that's where God is

When It Leaves One

it remains in the other

this will always be so
but there is not always
there is not "GOD"

just the moving
and the breathing
that are God

The phone call isn't God, I thought. The movement in my
fingers that makes the phone call is God. "It's beautiful," I said,
when Heather's groggy voice answered after the fifth ring.
"Denver?"
"It's just gorgeous, Heather. Breathtaking, really." I ran my
finger down a page over the words of her poem. "It's like a little
prayer…a religious tract, but then not."
"What are you talking about?"
I swallowed. "Your poem. Your God, tomato, mother poem."
I took a breath. "It's so damn good." I shook my head. "It's so good."
She was quiet, and then, "That really means more than you
can know."
I flipped back to the beginning of the poem. "I must have
read it like three—"
"Hold on a minute," she said.
I heard her moving in the bed. Other noises. I
imagined some guy lying next to her, waking up, wondering
who was calling.

I heard the flick of her lighter and her inhaling close to the mouthpiece. "I just needed to open a window," she said, exhaling, her voice excited. "Do you really think it's good? I mean, really?"

I laughed. "It's in the *Kenyon Review*, for Christsake. What's it matter if I think it's good?"

She sucked in a drag and then let it out. "It matters."

"It's the best thing you've ever written. It's poetry...really poetry." I pushed my hand back through my hair. "And the form— I mean, all of it—it's exactly the way it needs to be said. It can't be said any other way than the way you've written it."

She thanked me again.

"The letter, too, the one you enclosed. That was really..." I touched the word God in her poem. "The letter—well, not the letter—but the writing of the letter, the movement it took to write the letter...that's God, too."

"You really read it," she said. "I mean, really read the poem."

"I did," I said. "Three times. Twice out loud. And I just love the premise, the idea that this girl is just making a tomato sandwich and thinking about her mother and everything that came together to make that moment—the found moments, the Godness behind all of it." I shook my head. "It's just beautiful. I mean, sublime, really."

She laughed. "Sublime?"

"Seriously. Fucking sublime."

"Like I said in the letter, I don't think I could have written it without you...without you in my head."

"What you just said, right there, that's not God. But, the urge—the emotion—and then the saying...that's God."

"Alright, alright. Don't make fun of it."

"I'm not making fun of it. I'm seeing with it," I said. "It's true."

We talked for awhile longer. She told me about Ragdale and what her residency had been like. "There were quite a few younger writers there. After a few days, a lot of them turned out to be jerks. All they could talk about was writing...and not really even about writing so much as about who they knew and what journals had accepted their work."

"I'm not surprised."

She laughed. "That's what I thought you'd say." I heard her light another cigarette. "There were nice ones, too, Denver. They weren't all jerks. You like to do that, you know. You put people in compartments, and there they stay."

In the past, what she said would have started an argument. The way she said it, though, she wasn't being confrontational. She was just telling me the truth. I'd misjudged Vance. I'd even misjudged my father. I nodded. "I guess I could work on that."

She told me about the night she sat at Arthur Mervin's table for dinner. "He's in his sixties, but he looks so much older," she said. She said one younger poet kept asking Mervin what percentage of poems should be previously published in a manuscript before it's sent out as a book. Mervin kept ignoring the question. "Eventually he turned to him and said, 'Young man, the natural world is asphyxiating, and its fate will be our fate. Seems to me that as a poet you might have bigger questions burning in your skull.'" She took in another drag and then exhaled again. "The poor guy," Heather said. "He just turned red." She said that it wasn't long before everyone at the table was talking about simultaneous submissions policies and whether or not anyone paid attention to them. Then, she said, the conversation turned to marketing and how it would be suicide for a poet not to be on Facebook.

"Mervin excused himself. He'd barely touched his food." She said he left the retreat two days earlier than planned. They'd heard from an assistant director that he'd left a note that said he was "sick at heart." The executive director denied that any such note was written and said only that Mervin had fallen suddenly ill. Heather said that they were able to get a well-known poet from Chicago to fill in for one of the readings that Mervin was supposed to give.

While Heather talked about Mervin, I heard my father roll up to sitting in his bed. He let out a labored sigh, and then the floor creaked under him. Still holding the phone to my ear, I stood and stretched my arm to my light switch. I sat in the dark, listening to her and to him. He shuffled down the groaning hallway. Then came the sound of his weak, intermittent stream of urine. He pushed out the last few feeble salvos and then flushed. By the time the toilet tank had refilled itself, he was back in bed, rolling around to find a comfortable position for his old bones.

Heather asked me some questions about my summer. I didn't tell her much. A little bit about my job, about Ricky and Vance. I was thankful that she didn't ask me about any poems I might have been working on. Maybe she simply knew that I wasn't. I didn't tell her how I'd been knocked out and robbed. I never ended up telling anyone about it. I guess not until now.

I did tell her about the Roethke House.

"You need to do something," she said.

"I tried. It looks like it's a done deal." I held my hand splayed out in front of me toward the gray light of the window. It looked like the shadow puppet of a hand. "Nobody cares about that house, anyway."

"You do," she said.

"I don't think that's enough."

My father's house pinged in the walls, settling further into its foundation.

Heather asked me if I remembered marching with the graduate students.

It took me a moment to remember what she was talking about. Then it came to me. Back in October, the teaching assistants had been asking the university for more money. They claimed that their pay was close to slave labor. For a week the student newspaper ran stories that showed how little U of M's graduate teaching assistants were paid compared to other Big Ten schools and how in many cases they had more responsibilities than other school's TAs.

On a cold Thursday afternoon in November, the TAs marched in protest outside one of the administration buildings. I skipped an afternoon of workshop to join them. It must have been something like twenty degrees outside. We crunched through the fallen leaves shouting slogans about fair pay and fair working conditions. Despite the cold, one girl showed up in her Hooters uniform with a protest sign that read "Exploited TA Exploiting Her T&A." I made my own sign the night before: "Undergraduates For Under-paid Graduate Students." I'd organized about twenty other people to come with me. A few of them skipped classes, too. Campus police got support from the Ann Arbor city police. A group of about thirty of them, hard-mouthed and resolute, spread out and kept an eye on us. The protest stayed peaceful and broke up after a few hours.

"I should have gone with you," Heather said.

"What?"

"That afternoon. I should have gone to the protest with you. It bothers me that I didn't."

I reminded her that she liked Professor Schwartz's critiques better than I did, probably because Professor Schwartz was always so honest and accurate about my poetry. "This isn't a poem," she said, holding up the third one I'd brought in to workshop, "It's an essay broken up into little lines. An essay full of beautiful sentiment, yes, but an essay nonetheless." She'd set the poem in front of me, smiling. "Get some poetry into your poems, Mr. Hoptner."

"I still should have gone," Heather said.

112

I shrugged. "I don't see how it mattered. The administration didn't budge, and the TAs eventually lost their steam for protesting."

"It did matter, though," she whispered.

In the distance I heard not one, but six or seven motorcycles kicked to growling in the parking lot of the Red Horse. I imagined them taking off, spreading across the wounded cityscape like riders of the Apocalypse.

"Where are you right now, Heather? Are you at another retreat?"

She told me she was staying with her parents. "Just for a few weeks." She said that she had a late offer from another school that she needed to think over.

Her parents lived in Fort Wayne, Indiana, less than four hours from Saginaw. Thinking of it, I rubbed my fingers over the lump on the back of my head. It really only hurt if I touched it. "What are you doing until then?"

"Denver!" My father's voice startled me coming through the wall. The motorcycles must have woken him. "Can you hang up now? It's after two o'clock in the morning."

I held my hand over the mouthpiece. "Okay, Dad. Sorry."

He told me that I could call back tomorrow. "It's just getting late, now."

I came back on the phone. "I guess I should let you go. I'm keeping my dad awake."

She said that she was glad that I called, and she thanked me again for what I said about her poem.

"I didn't say anything that wasn't true."

Before saying goodbye, she told me to call her again when I had the chance.

"I will," I said.

I lay in bed looking at the silhouettes of tree branches through my window and listening to my father adjusting himself in his bed. Something in the attic scurried across to the other side of my ceiling...something nocturnal waking to its activity.

Waking.

The phone call had gone well. Still, I was glad my Dad cut me off when he did. In his half-sleep, he must have had a paternal sense of the hazard I was heading toward. I was about to suggest to Heather that she use a couple of her free days to come up to Saginaw and visit. That would have been a mistake. I could hear her: "Come up there? I'll have to think about— but, hey, you were saying you were thinking about moving to Portland? That sounds like a good idea for you. Let's talk about that."

Exhausted, I snapped my eyes open every time I felt myself close to sleep, fearing that somehow I wouldn't wake up after my blow to the head. Faces kept passing through my mind. Roethke's forlorn visage. Abby's resolved countenance. Heywood's disappointed frown.

Drifting in and out of sleep, I half-dreamed of Arthur Mervin. I knelt at the doorstep of his cabin in the Rockies, promising to do something about his sick heart. He reached down and touched my shoulder and told me to rise.

Blinking awake, I looked around in the darkness, unable for a moment to place myself. The softly ringing bells that filled the room turned out to be my neighbor's wind chimes twisting in breezes that were scouting ahead of a new front of weather.

I was in my boyhood bedroom under my father's roof.

Arthur Mervin.

What a strange, strange dream.

13.

Wearing my dad's sports coat, I was sitting at a table in the River View Hotel's largest conference room—the room they used for luncheons. I smoothed my damp palms down the thighs of my pants and took deep breaths, trying to get my heart to slow. My nametag, with the last name hidden under my lapel, read: Blake Russell, Muskegon. I guessed that someone named Blake would be a younger guy like me. I also guessed that since Blake's nametag was still at the conference's check-in area at eleven o'clock that morning that he probably wasn't coming. While at U of M, I'd gone to a few writers conferences. I had seen how at the end of the day there were always a couple dozen nametags that hadn't been claimed, people who had registered and then for whatever reason hadn't shown up.

I hoped for some kind of travel problems for Blake. Not a car accident or anything really bad, just a minor breakdown on the highway that would, at the least, keep him delayed until after lunch.

The banquet porters had set the room up for over one hundred people to eat. The wait staff was walking around checking to make sure every place setting had silverware or that the water pitchers were full. I only recognized a few of them. From what I could tell, none of them recognized me. They were probably too busy to notice that a guy who had just recently been working as a temp for the maintenance department was now attending the conference that the hotel had spent weeks getting ready for. Ricky came in at one point carrying a step ladder. I bent over and made like I was tying my shoe, even though I didn't have any laces. I peeked up over the edge of the table and watched him. He went up the ladder, changed out a dead light bulb, and was gone in less than two minutes. He didn't even look in my direction. He was too busy checking his phone for texts. I smiled and shook my head.

A dozen or so other people from the conference were walking around the room. Some recognized each other and waved or introduced themselves. When the first three or four had come in, I noticed right away that they liked to mingle. I slipped out to the lobby and grabbed a *Free Press*. When I got back to my seat, I opened up to the business section and tried to look like I was really absorbed in an article. In truth, the words were just a blur, little lines of dead sugar ants squashed across the page. It seemed to be working, though. Nobody went out of their way to talk to me.

A half hour earlier, I'd had the room to myself. They had Blake Russell seated at a table near a wall and not far from the ladies bathroom. Nobody noticed when I switched his name placard to another table that was much closer to the podium. A guy from Detroit named Ted Tomlinson was going to be sitting in Blake's seat. The way my heart was smacking around in my chest, I figured somebody from the wait staff would hear it, but they just went on with dealing out forks and knives and adjusting centerpieces.

The breakout sessions were ending. More and more people were coming into the lunch room. The place hummed with all the conversations and light laughing. A man with silver hair and a really nice suit cruised a circle around my table, found his name, and then sat down. I nodded to him, swallowing my heart back into place. He picked up his fork and turned it in the light. A few seconds later, he did the same with his knife.

"Is that the trick?" he asked, pushing his thinning gray hair into place. "Pretend to read the paper, and then you don't have to talk to any of these jackasses?"

I shrugged, feeling a stinging heat race along the base of my neck. I figured he knew the actual Blake Russell, or at least knew that there was no way in hell that someone my age would be sitting at the head table.

He smiled and set down his spoon. "Well, let me have the sports section at least. I can only inspect my silverware for so long before somebody guesses that I have dementia and calls for my resignation."

Nodding, I peeled out the sports pages and gave them to him. Shaking them open, he smiled in a way that suggested we were now friends, co-conspirators in a covert operation that involved not having to talk to anyone. He wanted quiet because he'd probably heard everything that could be said at a conference like this. He looked important. There were probably a lot of assholes just itching to schmooze with him. I'd seen it at writing conferences—young writers zeroing in on the most respected writers in the room, lubricating their brown noses with proctologist jelly, hoping to slip in their obsequious remarks as painlessly and productively as possible.

I had different reasons for not wanting anyone to talk to me. I wasn't avoiding ass-kisses and suck-ups. I was avoiding everybody.

I was an uninvited guest, a mole among the insurance agents, infiltrating in the name of poetry.

That morning I'd driven to the hotel around nine o'clock to pick up my last paycheck. There were more cars in the parking lot than I'd ever seen. They had a huge sign in the lobby welcoming the conference attendees. That's when I finally saw the name: Welcome Hartland Insurance Company.

It was only a few seconds later that the bell chimed, the elevator doors slid open, and the man himself stepped out surrounded by three or four other men in suits.

D.W. Wallace.

They walked past me. Mr. Wallace listened while the other men talked. He looked older than in the pictures I'd seen of him. I guessed that he was in his late seventies. His eyes, though... his eyes were the same. Gray and piercing—more like a wolf's than a man's. His silver hair was receded almost to his crown. He wore it longer and swept back on the sides and pulled off the look in a way that other men couldn't.

I first learned about him in a literature course I'd taken called American Poets Since World War II. As a poet, he'd been at his peak in the late sixties and much of the seventies. He won a National Book Award for his collection, *Driving with One Headlight*. Most poetry anthologies had at least one poem by him, usually "My Father Pruning at Dusk." Unlike many of his contemporaries, he never taught. His grandfather, a Detroiter, had started Hartland Insurance and when he died the reigns had been taken up by his father. D. W. Wallace worked under his dad for years while still writing poems and building a reputation as a poet.

Even at the height of his poetic success, he never quit Hartland or even took a hiatus. Eventually his father passed away, and D.W. became CEO of the company. There was a famous quote attributed to him: "I write poetry to stay alive; I sell insurance so my family can eat." As far as I knew, he was still writing. A few years before I'd read a poem by him in *The New Yorker*. It stuck out to me because it was actually funny, something I didn't remember finding in any of his earlier work.

In any of the bios I'd read about him, one fact was always included. He'd been a student of Roethke's. One of his other less anthologized poems was titled "First Class"—a long poem describing Roethke's manic, intimidating, and sometimes frightening behavior on the first day of class. I still remembered the last lines:

117

and so we sat for a moment
even after he'd left the room,
feeling the semester ahead,
as though we were barometers
measuring the pressure
of what we would have to do
to keep him from loathing us.
It'd only been an hour
and still we wanted his favor,
like children of a hard father.
We loved him already
for everything we knew
he'd give us, even as the giving
slowly maimed him.

After seeing him in the lobby, I didn't even bother picking up my check. I went back out to my father's truck and started for home. I needed to get the right clothes on, or at least as close as I could come between my father's wardrobe and mine. I needed to talk to D.W. Wallace. I needed to get him to listen. If anyone would care about what was happening at the Roethke House, he would. He knew other poets, too…other students of Roethke's. The man who had written "First Class" couldn't possibly hear the details and then do nothing.

Outside of the conference room on one of the patios, a group of men and women were smoking. The backside of the hotel looked nice where a lush half acre of lawn, dotted with pine trees, sloped down to Lake Linton. Across the lake, even the east end of Ojibway Island seemed picturesque. From where they were smoking, they could look and see the topmost floors of the Second National Bank Building downtown looking majestic in the noon sun.

One of the women—the way she tilted her neck to exhale—reminded me of Heather. I hadn't spoken to her since the week before when I called her about her poem. I hadn't done much since that night besides work and finally, after my dad's badgering, renew my license.

The room was filling up quickly. Three other men, each impeccably dressed, had found their name placards and sat down at the table where I was sitting. My recent friend had folded up the sports section and started talking with the new arrivals. They seemed his equals, and their conversation was easy and down-to-earth, mainly centering around grandchildren and family. They were men with money, and they had good stories to share about sons and daughters finishing law school or receiving promotions. One man begrudgingly reported that his son was still in New York trying to make a go of an acting career. "We're keeping the basement ready for him," he said, and the others laughed.

Nobody said anything to me, even though I'd also folded up my paper. I glanced to my right a few times just to double check that it was indeed D.W. Wallace's name in front of the place setting next to mine.

Across the room, I saw a man who looked very similarly dressed to the men sitting with me. Ted Tomlinson, I guessed. He was in the seat that had been reserved for Blake Russell. He looked perplexed. The young men sitting with him were smiling and talking at him. In between absently nodding to what they were saying, he craned his neck and looked around the room, perhaps replaying in his head what he might have said or done over the past six months that had relegated him to the cheap seats.

"Gentlemen," a smooth voice said above me and to my right. "Oh, and you, too, Bill."

The men laughed.

D.W. Wallace pulled out his chair and sat down next to me. I slipped my trembling hands off the table and set them on my knees.

"Where's Tomlinson?" Mr. Wallace asked.

One of the men said that he'd seen him that morning.

"There he is over there," Mr. Wallace said, pointing, "sitting with some of the folks from the west side of the state."

I guessed that they were going to ask me to move. "Mr. Wallace," I started. It came out barely above a whisper.

"That's good thinking," Mr. Wallace said, pointing in Tomlinson's direction. "That's what we should all be doing…talking to some of the troops instead of boring each other."

They nodded, their faces showing the envy they had towards Tomlinson's initiative.

Mr. Wallace turned toward me. "Did he switch seats with you?"

"Maybe," I choked out, pointing at my name placard. "This is where somebody put me."

"D.W. Wallace," he said, extending his thin, bony hand.

"Yes, Mr. Wallace," I stammered, putting my hand in his warm, dry grip. "I know who you are."

He smiled. "I wish I could say the same of you."

"Oh," I said. "Blake, sir." I pealed back my lapel to show him. I looked, too. I didn't remember the last name. "Blake Russell. From Muskegon."

119

He pumped my hand once and then pulled his from my cold, sweaty grip. "Very good to meet you." He asked me how things were in Muskegon.

"Good," I said.

He looked at me like he wanted more, as though he expected me to talk about how we were dealing with some loophole in a life insurance policy.

"What do you do for us over in Muskegon?"

Before I had to fake my way through something, the waitress arrived and started setting Caesar salads in front of us. If I would have had a ring, I would have gotten down on one knee and proposed to her.

We started eating. One of the men brought up a new marketing campaign that targeted newly divorced mothers. Apparently, many of them didn't have the insurance they needed. They were an untapped demographic.

At one point, Mr. Wallace leaned over to me. "Don't care for your salad?"

If I would have eaten anything, I most likely would have thrown up on the table. I told him that I didn't like the dressing.

He agreed with me that it wasn't very good.

The waitress came again and cleared our plates. It wasn't long after that she was back, setting down the main course of seared chicken breasts, wild rice, and asparagus.

The talk about insurance died off. Each man committed himself to working at the entrée. Not wanting to stand out, I risked a few bites and was able to keep them down.

The entire room was clinking with forks hitting plates and murmuring with voices and laughter.

I took a deep breath and turned to Mr. Wallace. "I've always admired your poetry," I said. "You studied with Roethke, didn't you?"

He was chewing a piece of chicken. He swallowed and then turned and looked at me. "Is your family of German descent?"

I didn't know what he was talking about. Hoptner was German. I didn't think Russell was. "I don't think so," I said.

He nodded and then looked at the men around the table. "If you get a chance to circulate to the branch heads, get the word out about the Post-Loss Liability session tomorrow morning at eight. I know it's early, but I think any agent with less than three years experience should be there."

The other men nodded in agreement.

"I may forget to mention it during my talk. We've had a lot of new hires statewide in the past two years."

He looked over at me and poked his finger into my arm. "Be a good session for you, I'd imagine. Keep you out of any potential hot water."

I nodded.

The man who had borrowed the sports section spoke up. "I'm sure I'll have a lot of people this afternoon. I'm giving that update on some of the new graduated competency requirements coming out of Lansing for recreational boating and how that could affect existing policies. I'll mention it then, D.W."

Each man in turn mentioned when, in the course of the conference, he would have the chance to plug the session on Post-Loss Liability.

We were halfway through dessert before I had a chance to bend Mr. Wallace's ear again.

"I really like your poem 'First Class.'"

He looked at me and smiled. "Thank you."

"It must have been something else to have Roethke as a—"

"Young man," Mr. Wallace said, putting his hand on my shoulder, "you're talking to me about poetry."

I looked into his icy, haunting eyes.

"This is an insurance conference. We are here to talk about insurance and insurance only." He smiled. "Never forget where you are." Using my shoulder, he pushed himself to standing.

The room slowly went quiet as people noticed him.

It took me a few seconds to remember how to swallow.

"I apologize, everybody, for interrupting your dessert," Mr. Wallace said, raising his voice, "but I have a few things to say before you run off to blissfully attend your afternoon sessions." He pointed his finger around the room with mock authority. "And you will do it blissfully. I'll know it if you don't."

People laughed. Mr. Wallace started for the podium. I stood up, making eye contact with nobody. I threaded my way through the tables and chairs.

I was nearly to the door when somebody held his hand against my chest and stopped me.

I looked up into Ted Tomlinson's pale, chiseled face. He was a good six inches taller than me.

"How is it that you're sitting at the head table?" he asked.

Mr. Wallace's voice was coming through the speakers around the room in a cadence that suggested he was delivering somber news.

I tried to step around Tomlinson, but he stepped with me. His hand was still on my chest, hot through my shirt. He was strong.

"Hmm?"

"I don't know," I said. "That's where they put—"

He pushed my lapel aside and read the name. "That's funny. The young men I'm sitting with say you aren't Blake Russell." His eyebrows narrowed. "Who the hell—"

"Isn't that right, Ted?" Mr. Wallace said.

Mr. Tomlinson looked up toward the podium. "What?"

Mr. Wallace smiled and leaned to the mic. "I said you're showing those of us with a little more winter in our hair that it's still good to mingle."

His grip loosened on my chest. "That's right," he shouted. I used the opportunity to slip past him.

Jogging down the long hallway that went past the doors of other smaller conference rooms, I looked back a few times. Nobody was following me.

The carpet ended at the tile of the lobby.

"Denver?"

It was a blonde girl that worked the front desk some mornings. We had spoken once for a few minutes in the break room. At the time she was taking a summer English course and struggling in it. We had talked about how I could tutor her. I gave her my number, but she never called.

She looked at my sports coat and dress pants. "What are you—"

I bolted for the men's room. Standing over one of the sinks, I splashed water on my face and took deep breaths.

It didn't help.

Lurching toward it, I opened the first stall, knelt, and lost everything that I'd thought I'd be able to hold down.

14.

I was standing outside of D.W. Wallace's room with a pillow under my arm. I could hear his television on the other side of the door. It sounded like a news program. I glanced up and down the hallway at the other doors. It was some time after eight o'clock. People were either at dinner or back from dinner. I guessed that a lot of them were settling into bed. They had that early meeting in the morning about Post-Loss Liability. The last thing I wanted to do was run into Ted Tomlinson. He would remember me, I was sure.

I'd already been home, written a letter, torn up the letter, and then driven back to the hotel. I had wanted to slip the letter under his door. Before I was even halfway finished with writing it, I stopped. I just didn't trust my own words. Most of the writing I'd done over the past year had fallen far short of what I thought it capable…of what I'd imagined in my head.

After destroying the letter, I decided that I wasn't going to do anything. I had tried at lunch, and it had amounted to nothing. I went downstairs to listen to a ball game with Dad. He told me that the Tigers weren't playing. It's funny. If they had been playing, I probably wouldn't have done anything. I would have listened to the game, had a beer or two, and then gone to bed. Instead, Dad went through all of the stations and then announced that there was nothing worth our time. We talked for awhile and came up with a list of things I could do around the house since I was done working. We'd had a few nights of heavy rain. I asked him about the walls in the basement.

"What?"

"Remember the walls that you said were compromised? You were going to plug them with hydraulic cement. Did it work?"

He smiled and nodded. "Dry as a bone down there," he said.

"Well, that's good."

It wasn't long after that he told me he was going to bed. He hadn't felt good for most of the day he said.

Going up the steps, he put his hand on his left knee and used it like a cane to get the right leg up each step. He made little grunting noises. I was filled with the urge to apologize. I hadn't meant to be so difficult. And then, after Mom died—the way I just left him alone with his grief. For what it was worth, I wanted to tell him that I loved him.

The moment had passed. He had already disappeared upstairs.

His footsteps came through the ceiling, creaking in the joists. It was a word I had learned from him. Joists. It was a good word.

He got into bed.

Outside, it was still light. After a minute, I called Heywood.

"Hello?"

"Hey man, what's going—"

"Hello?!"

"Heywood? It's Den—"

"I'm just playin'. You got my voicemail. Make some words, leave your digits."

I hung up and sat for awhile watching the dust floating in the column of sunlight coming through the west-facing window. After some thinking, I went upstairs and put on a pair of blue jeans. Dad's snoring came through the wall.

One way or another, I was going to talk to D.W. Wallace. We were going to talk about poetry. More specifically, we were going to talk about Roethke...and Roethke's house.

I drove to the hotel with a loose plan in my head. The woman who worked the front desk in the evening only knew that I worked in the maintenance department. She didn't know that my last day had been the week before. I'd heard that she was in her forties and had devoted herself to the hotel like a nun once she'd left her husband. He'd been sleeping around.

When I asked for the key to the shop, she didn't even hesitate. Once I was down there, I changed into my uniform shirt, tucked it into my jeans, and grabbed a pass key. I wrote a few things on a work order and then started for the lobby.

Handing the shop key back to her, I peeked at the front desk clerk's nametag. "Hey Linda. Can you tell me what room a Mr. Wallace is in?"

She nodded and then keyed his last name into her computer. Running her finger halfway down the screen, she stopped on the information she needed, and then looked at me. "Why?" she asked.

I had figured that she wasn't going to give me what I wanted easily. They were trained to keep room information on a need-to-know basis. I'd planned for it. I told her that Mr. Wallace had talked to me in the parking lot earlier that day while I was picking up cigarette butts. "He said that his air conditioning unit was making a rattling noise," I lied. Taking the work order from my pocket, I showed her where I'd minutes before scrawled, "Check Mr. Wallace's air conditioning unit." I told her that I'd forgotten to get his room number. "Must be my day to forget," I said. "I was changing to go out tonight, and I found this in my back pocket." I waved the work order back and forth and smiled sheepishly. "I swear I'd forget my ass if it wasn't attached to my legs." That was one of my dad's lines. I hoped it wasn't too offensive.

Fortunately, she laughed before giving me a room number up on the sixth floor.

I slipped the work order back into my pocket.

My heart jumped when Linda picked up the phone and put it to her ear. "I'll let him know that you're coming up," she said.

A sweaty heat raced into my palms as she punched in the number. What could I say that wouldn't look questionable?

"Mr. Wallace? This is Linda at the front desk. One of our gentlemen from the maintenance department is coming up to your room. Is this a convenient time?"

If he didn't say yes, I was screwed.

"Oh, yes, of course, sir. He'll be right up." She asked me to wait a minute and then disappeared into a room behind the front desk. When she came out again, she was holding a pillow. "This works out great," she said. "He was just about to call for an extra pillow, and the night porter is out in the van at the airport waiting to pick up a guest." She handed me the pillow. "Now don't forget this in the elevator," she said, smiling and giving the pillow a little wiggle.

My original plan had been to open his door, knock, and then announce that I was there to check on a problem in the bathroom. I imagined that he'd be lying on the bed and wouldn't bother to get up. Thanks to Linda's phone call, I had to somehow give him the damn pillow.

The bell to the elevator chimed down the hallway. Imagining Ted Tomlinson coming around the corner, I slid the pass key through the lock and opened the door to Wallace's room. "Maintenance, sir," I said, relieved to see his feet at the end of the room's bed closest to the window. He was watching one of the televisions that I'd installed.

"Come in." The door to the bathroom was immediately on my right. I took a few steps past it, tossed the pillow onto the first bed, and then retreated back into the bathroom. I was from the maintenance department after all. He surely didn't expect me to fluff the pillow and tuck it behind his head.

I heard him rise from the bed and then a moment later lay down on it again. "Thank you," he called.

I told him that I was going to check his toilet. "The last guest in this room reported a problem with the toilet tank refilling itself in the middle of the night," I said. "I'm just going to look at the flapper."

"Well, I haven't heard anything," he said.

My hands were shaky as I removed the top of the tank. I told him that it might be a slow leak. "We call it phantom flushing."

"Phantom flushing," he repeated. "That's a good phrase."

I smiled. He was thinking like a poet again. Maybe after five o'clock he was able to detach himself from the insurance thing.

Maybe I had a chance.

I took a deep breath. Stooped over the toilet tank, plunging my arm, pretending to look for a problem that didn't exist, I tried to think of something to say, something that would eventually lead us to Roethke and the Roethke House. The water was cold. I lifted the slimy flapper and water started to rush into the bowl. I set the flapper back into place and the water stopped. "Are you here with the conference?" I had to play a little dumb.

He confirmed what I already knew.

"Is everything going good?" I figured that poor grammar might be more authentic.

"As well as can be expected," he said. Then, a few seconds later, "Of course, this phantom flushing issue has me feeling a little haunted."

There was a lightheartedness in his voice. I laughed. "Trying to exorcise the ghost as we speak, sir," I said, drying my hand on my pants. I was likely going a little too far. Probably not the banter he expected out of a guy from the maintenance department.

He turned down the volume on the television. "Well, I'm certain you'll flush it out."

I laughed again, but let him have the last word. "Hopefully you'll have a little time to get out and explore Saginaw while you're here." About three weeks ago all of the hotel employees—even temporary employees like me—had to attend a mandatory two-hour meeting about how we should speak with the conference guests. Part of the meeting included a talk with a woman from the Chamber of Commerce. She urged us to find a way to mention area attractions. "This is an opportunity for the entire city," she said, "not just the hotel."

Mr. Wallace informed me that his itinerary was quite full.

I stirred my hand through the water in the tank, just to sound like I was doing something. "Well, if you can get out, you might want to check out the zoo. Or the Japanese Tea House. Both are just right down the road." I waited a second. "Oh, there's also the Theodore Roethke House."

He was quiet for a moment. "What did you say?"

The springs of the bed groaned when he sat up. I had him. He was interested. "The Theodore Roethke House," I said again, reaching for the handle and flushing the toilet. I raised my voice above the watery din. "He was a pretty famous poet from Saginaw."

"Yes, I know," he said.

His shaken voice was right behind me in the doorway of the bathroom. My intestines went icy. I turned slowly on my knees and looked up at him.

His fiery eyes were staring into mine. He was holding his belt with the buckle dangling down. "I thought I recognized your voice. Not many people pronounce Roethke's last name correctly."

I held up my hands. Something was racing through me, like I was on speed. "I know, right? I know. This seems really crazy, I'll bet."

"It seems illegal," he said.

I shook my head. "I know. I know. But I do work here. I mean, I did. I just wanted—"

"Don't move," he said, rearing back his hand with the belt in it.

I dropped back to my knees. "Look. Seriously, I'm harmless. I'm not crazy. You don't have to— I know it seems crazy…me at lunch and then now in your room. But, I'm not crazy. I just…I need to talk to you. I need to talk to you about Roethke, about his house."

He stared at me. His fingers pulsed on the belt, assuring his grip.

I pumped my palms at him pleadingly. "I know you were one of his students," I said. "One of his best-known students. I read your poem, 'First Class.' I love it…just love it. I just wanted to talk to you, just for five minutes. Then, whatever you want. Call the police or whatever. It just didn't seem like there was any other way to talk…I mean, after today, after I tried to talk to you, and then—This just seemed like the only way. It's stupid, I know. Crazy. But I couldn't… I mean, I couldn't just let you leave town without even trying. I wrote a letter telling you about it, telling you everything. It wasn't enough. I can't really write. I needed to talk to you face-to-face. I thought if I could just tell you—"

127

"Tell me what." His voice was stern.

"About the Roethke House, his boyhood home. There was a fire, and now…I don't know. It seems so stupid. But, it's this museum, right? It's this place where people can—"

"I know about it, young man," he said, nodding. "I gave a fundraising reading there in the late nineties just after Annie Waters purchased it."

"Abby," I said.

He nodded. "Right. Abby Waters." He looked at me for a moment. His hand with the belt in it was relaxed at his side. "You said there was a fire?"

"Yeah, yeah. I mean, it didn't burn the place down. But they can't afford…it's just that this inspector from the city came. They don't have the money to bring the place up to code. They're going to have to sell it. It won't be a museum…or anything."

He rubbed his hand on his forehead. "Get up," he said. "Just get up and come in here." He walked back into the room.

I stood and followed him.

He turned off the television and then sat on the bed. He motioned toward a chair. "Sit down," he said.

I pulled the chair out and sat. "I'm really sorry," I said. "I'm sorry if I scared you or anything."

"What's your real name?"

"Denver Hoptner."

He smiled after a moment and pointed. "You do have some German in you, then."

I nodded.

"All of this…crashing our conference luncheon and then showing up in my room? It was all about the Roethke House?"

I nodded, touching my fingers along the surface of the desk. I told him about working for the hotel and how I recognized his company's name. "I knew when I saw you this morning that I had to talk to you."

Sitting with his hands on his knees, he asked me questions about the fire. I told him what I knew. About the insurance. About the board of the Patrons of Roethke. About the landlord in Saginaw who wanted the house and the guy in Bay City. I told him about Abby and how she seemed so worn down by all of it.

"I remember meeting her," he said, scratching his upper lip. "She had the passion of ten people. Even then, though, I knew if she didn't get people behind her—and money—that her whole vision for the house wouldn't go anywhere." He shook his head. "This is

America. Passion alone doesn't get you very far." He gave a low whistle. "Twenty thousand dollars. That's no small sum."

I nodded.

He smiled, rubbing his palms over his knees. "You didn't think that I would donate that much, did you?"

I told him I didn't know what I thought.

"I'm not in a position to donate that kind of money, no matter what the cause."

A door opened out in the hallway and then closed again.

"I don't know," I said, "I thought maybe you could help get word out to the poetry world, or at least other people who were his students."

He rubbed his chin, nodding thoughtfully. "Well, of course, James Wright is deceased. He was probably the student who went on to the most fame. Richard Hugo." He shrugged. "Dead." He pointed at me. "There's Carolyn Kizer. She's still alive...and has money, I hear. Oh, and Tess Gallagher, Ray Carver's widow, and a fine poet herself. There's James Knisely, the novelist." He pushed his hand through his hair. "There are others." He nodded. "Many, I'm sure."

He stood up and walked over to the window and looked out at the speckled lights of Saginaw. "Others, too, even if they weren't Roethke's students, they might give. *Poetry* magazine inherited an absolute windfall of money, like 200 million dollars or some ridiculous amount. Might be worth a phone call to their foundation."

I was sitting behind him, nodding at his every word, silently willing him into other avenues.

He was quiet, just staring out into the night. "You know," he said, almost whispering, "I can safely say that I would have never been a poet if it wasn't for Roethke." He touched the glass, and his reflection in it touched him back. "I was just a kid running away from what seemed like a predetermined future. I got out to Seattle and picked poetry because it seemed as far removed from the insurance business as I could get. I probably chose it to spite my father. But then I got in there, with Roethke. The man made me love language. He made me want to make poetry a part of my life...a big part."

He turned and looked at me with his canine-gray eyes. "It wasn't always good for me. I idolized him too much, read everything he ever wrote. I ended up writing like him—practically copying him—and didn't even know it. When my first book *REM Sleep* came out, the reviewers picked up on it. Eight reviews, and every one of them mentioned echoes of Roethke. One reviewer, Jack Winslow, a little prick at *The Detroit Free Press*, actually called the poems derivative.

129

That was a kick to the stomach, but I needed it. It took me two solid years to shake Roethke's influence. When I did though, when I'd released myself, one thing remained…that love of language. Except I was loving it on my terms. I'd found a way to sing with my own voice." He pointed at me. "But, Roethke, he got all of it started. I owe him that."

He smiled. "Jack Winslow played his part, too. In fact, I knew he was a scotch drinker, and I sent a hundred-dollar bottle over to the paper for him when I won the National Book Award. He probably had no idea why, but he deserved my thanks, too, prick or not. And he is a little prick. Still."

"How did you end up working for Hartland…for your father?" I asked, thinking of my own dad. I wondered if I'd dropped out of teaching just to spite him. When he asked me what kind of job I'd get by studying how to be a poet, I said, "I'm not really all that worried about ever getting a job." I said it because I knew it would grind his gears. He hung up on me, which was what I'd wanted.

Mr. Wallace turned back to the window, back to his reflection. "When I finished my degree, I knew I didn't want to teach. I'd seen how it drained Roethke. Many of the other students were applying to graduate schools. MFA programs were popping up all over the place. I didn't want that, though. I just wanted to write. I figured I'd learned what I needed to learn about poetry, which was probably my mistake. I came back to Detroit and told my old man that I was going to be a poet. He told me that he figured poets needed to eat, too. He let me work as a claims adjuster until…'you find something else,' he said.

"So, I worked in the day and wrote at night." He pointed at me. "The claims work, though, that became important, too. I was meeting with widows who were helpless without their husbands, afraid even, or with people who had lost their homes—everything—to fires. The insurance…it brought them some peace. There was nobility in the business. Necessity. A lot of those early claims adjusting experiences ended up in *Driving with One Headlight*. I mined those experiences for truth. I came to realize that insurance was something that I could never leave. Like poetry, it was in my blood."

He shook his head. "In that first book, I was trying to write about the natural world, like Roethke had. I was driving out to the metro parks and forcing myself to see something in those little manmade lakes, the forests…forcing myself to write about it." He shook his head again. "I was a city boy. And, really, a suburban boy. I had my own dirt I needed to get down into, not Roethke's dirt."

130

I sat listening to him. What was in my blood? Would I ever find my dirt?

He walked around the end of the bed and sat down again. "Roethke was a remarkable man. Truly. Not without his warts, but I've never met another like him." He looked up, tapping a finger just gently beneath his nose, his eyes far away. "And as a poet…my God. It's like he reinvented himself with every book. Read his greenhouse poems and then read *The Far Field*. Stylistically, length, tone—all of it. It's like two different men, but the same dirt is in there. I don't think enough has been said about that, about how hard that is. It's hard enough to find one voice, one way to get at things. He had so many."

I nodded. "And he was from Saginaw."

"Of course."

I adjusted myself in the chair. "I mean, he did what he did in poetry even though he was from this place."

He looked at me with a furrowed brow. "Even though?"

"Well, yeah. I mean, he was from here and, still, he wrote this incredible— "

"Have you read his poetry?"

His eyes were piercing again—piercing into me. "Some," I said.

"Do really think he was a great poet despite being from Saginaw?" He breathed a sharp, little laugh and pointed at me. "He was a great poet because he was from Saginaw…because of the greenhouses, and the fields, the river…all of it."

I started to say something.

He interrupted. "There's so much Saginaw in his work. He may not have always loved the people, but he loved the place. Even when he was changing form or style, his childhood—his Saginaw childhood—was the well he went to again and again for his images."

I sat, listening.

"He may have left, but he never really left. And, he often came back. In the summers, he came and stayed. Writing…in that house. He wrote the poem 'The Lost Son' in that house." He stopped. "Have you read it? 'The Lost Son'?"

I shook my head.

"Oh," he said, "it's glorious. It's like a bonsai *Ulysses*."

I didn't tell him that I'd never read Joyce. Hopefully it was enough that I intended to read him some day.

Mr. Wallace kept talking. "He was on a Guggenheim Fellowship when he was working on that book. Still, he didn't travel. He stayed in Saginaw." He jabbed his finger rhythmically against the mattress. "He knew that's what would bring the poems out of him. That's where the poems were. That house…this place."

I wanted more than ever to save the place, that hothouse of so much poetic energy. "I didn't know," I said. "I thought once he went to college, he was gone."

He shook his head. "He came back to Saginaw quite a bit, sometimes to write and sometimes to recuperate from episodes of mental breakdown. Many of the poems in *Praise to the End!* were written in Saginaw too, or at least started here."

I brushed my hand back through my hair. "I had no idea."

"I think Saginaw was something solid for him, somewhere to roost and find his center again—at least until he met Beatrice." He looked thoughtful, as though discovering the idea for the first time. "He didn't come back much after her."

He stood up, walked over to the window, and then came back to the bed. He talked for a while longer about Roethke—about his love of tennis and cooking. His love of steaks. He told me about Roethke's car, the green Buick Special that Ted called The Flying Jukebox. "He bought that car in Saginaw, too."

He told me about Roethke's reputation as a womanizer. Once, at a party, he was doing his flirting routine with a fellow faculty member's wife. She motioned to a door and told him, "That's a bedroom. Let's go, Ted." Mr. Wallace laughed. "Roethke turned beat red and walked away. He was much more timid than all his bluster. Much more tender than his toughness. Much more sensitive than his callousness." He cleared his throat. "He was like any of us. He wore masks to stay safe."

I listened. Then, after awhile, Mr. Wallace began to yawn. He told me it was time for us to call it a night and that he had an early meeting in the morning. He stood up, knees popping. "By the way, I'll do it. I'll contact some poets, the Poetry Foundation. Soon as I get back to Detroit, I'll see what money I can drum up. Maybe it will be twenty thousand."

I stood. "Anything you can do would be great."

He pointed at the hotel stationary and pen on the desk. "Leave me your address," he said. "I'll send a check of my own, too. I think something like a thousand dollars would prime the pump."

I shook his hand, and he led me to the door, warm hand on my shoulder, and then opened it. "Be careful on your way out," he said. "If Ted Tomlinson sees you, I don't know what he might do." He grinned. "He holds grudges."

I smiled. "I'll keep my eyes open."

15.

After the burial, a half dozen people came back to the funeral home with me for the meatballs and rolls they provided. There was a guy in his thirties that had worked for Dad's contracting business. He wanted me to know what a good guy my dad had been as a boss. Then he left. A few guys from Dad's GM days were standing in a small circle, catching each other up. Heywood was there, but he was outside smoking.

Sitting on a couch by myself, I was still a little numb. I had a plate with three meatballs on my lap. They rolled through their own sauce. A woman from the funeral home had fixed the plate for me. I wasn't hungry.

I watched the skinny funeral director come through a door and walk over to me. He told me that he thought the service very reverential. I listened to myself agree with him.

"Your poem was a lovely tribute," he said, touching the tips of his long fingers together.

He stood until I made eye contact. Once I did, he smiled, nodded, and then walked away.

The pastor had asked me if I wanted to say anything at the service. I didn't guess that there would be anyone there who would say something. I told him that if it was okay, I would write a poem.

Before I read the poem, I said a few things. I mentioned that my dad was a good man and a hard worker. I said that he must have been a man of faith because he believed in the Detroit Tigers every year, no matter if they fell apart after the All-Star game or not. That got a few laughs. It wasn't long before I ran out of things to say. "I wish I would have known him better," I said. It got a few puzzled looks, but it was true. Then, I smoothed a piece of paper on the podium and began to read:

> My father, on his knees
> in the basement, crouching
> along the cinderblocks,
> his mind on spring run-off

and heavy April rains,
the way brick can eventually
become compromised,
letting the dampness in
to wear at everything.
He cemented the leaks,
forcing the water down
into the weeping tiles.
He knew a little something
about loving a foundation.
I was upstairs lying prone
with a book, thinking myself
so much smarter than he.
I hardly knew anything.
Only now do I feel
in his unexpected dying
just how much he had
to teach me about living.

I'm not sure how the poem went over. A few people were smiling at me when I looked up. There were words that weren't very poetic, like "compromised." It was his word, though, and I wanted it in there. Afterwards, when people were coming through a line to greet me, Vance stopped and told me how much he liked the poem.

"I could see him down there in that basement," he said. "And I really liked the part about him knowing how to love a foundation." He looked at me. "It was more than just loving the foundation of a house, wasn't it, that he was good at?"

I felt the tears coming. I blinked my eyes and told him that he still needed to show me one of his poems.

He squeezed my hand. "Will do, buddy," he said, and then moved on.

I blinked a few more times. Others came through and shook my hand and introduced themselves. After the third person, I regained my composure and held it together, even with the hugging.

Dad had died the same night that I talked to D.W. Wallace. I got home some time after ten o'clock. I paced around the kitchen, absently taking drinks from a beer and replaying in my mind how things had gone. I figured it was too late to call Abby. I called Heywood but only got his voicemail again.

I needed to tell somebody. I went upstairs, trying not to be loud and at the same time hoping to be loud enough. Standing in the hallway, I opened Dad's door. I was about to try to wake him up. Then, I thought better of it. There'd be plenty of time to tell him in the morning. He'd appreciate it more after a cup of his tar-black coffee. I closed his door carefully and tiptoed back down the hallway. I worked my way down the stairs, finding the sweet spots that didn't give any creak back to me. I just suddenly had it in my head that I shouldn't wake the poor guy up.

Downstairs, I grabbed another beer, and sat in his chair. To give my head something to do other than think about D.W. Wallace and the Roethke House, I turned on the radio. The Tigers were in the bottom of the third with the A's out west. That should have been my clue that something was seriously wrong with Dad. He studied the Tigers playing schedule the way a priest studies scripture. He never missed a game and certainly didn't make mistakes as to when they might be playing. I didn't dwell on it for long. I figured old age was finally catching up to his memory, having no idea that it was catching up to much more.

I woke up the next morning still in his chair. He wasn't up, so I figured it must have been very early. Outside, sunshine poured over everything. When I checked the microwave in the kitchen, it was quarter after nine. I looked in the driveway. The truck was there. I checked the backyard and the basement. Even as I made my way around the house, I already knew what I was going to find up in his bedroom. I had trouble taking a full breath.

I opened his door. He was a lump under the covers. "Dad?" I asked into the dimness. "Dad." I went to his bedside and reached out, finding with my fingers the cold that I somehow knew would be there. He was gone.

I went down to my knees and lay my head on his chest. I stayed that way for a long time. My hand stroked his hair. "Oh, Dad."

When I finally stood up, I pulled the blanket over his head, more watching my hands do it than anything. I took a few steps back and stumbled into a chair that he kept in his room for putting on his shoes. I sat looking at the stretch of him under the blankets. With the passing of one night, I was alone in the world. My parents both were only children. Their parents were dead. My mother had a cousin out in Idaho. We'd only heard from her once. It was an announcement that one of her boys was graduating from high school. My mom smacked my dad on the arm when he said, "Ah, she remembers us when she wants some dough for her kid." The cousin didn't come for my mother's funeral. Who, I wondered, would come for my father's?

The phone calls I needed to make were all official. I had nobody by blood to inform.

In the hours that followed finding it, my father's body was taken to a medical examiner. One of the officers that came was really kind. He asked me some questions and found out that I was the only living relative. He told me that I needed to select a funeral home and start the arrangements. After Mom died, Dad showed me where he kept his important papers. Going through them, I found that he'd already made preparations regarding his death. He'd bought a plan that covered his casket, a small ceremony, and his burial.

The medical examiner's report indicated that Dad had suffered a massive heart attack. "We'll deliver the body to the funeral home," the voice on the other end of the line told me.

"Okay," I said. The body. My father was "the body."

After that, the business of his death kept me going so much that I really didn't have time to think about him being gone. I went to the funeral home for what seemed like the better part of one day. The funeral director told me that I should go to the probate court the next day. I did, and spent hours on paperwork. We needed to find out how much Dad still owed for Mom's medical expenses.

I didn't want to go home at night. I tried the first night, but I didn't like the hollowness of the place. It made me think about what it must have been like for Dad when Mom died. Heywood let me sleep on the floor of his room at his mother's place. It was a basement bedroom, and he had his own ground-floor entrance.

The days went quickly. Before long I was at the funeral home receiving a couple dozen attendees, reciting a poem, watching my father's casket descend into the ground, and then sitting with lukewarm meatballs on my lap.

A man my father's age that I'd seen at the visitation, the service, and at the burial broke off from the GM group and stepped up to me where I sat on the couch. He was bald and had a bone-white trucker mustache. He offered his hand and told me how sorry he was for my loss.

"I'm Chuck Burns." He smiled. "Mind if I sit?" he asked, motioning to the spot next to me on the couch.

I set my plate on the coffee table and nodded for him to take a seat.

He rubbed his warm palm on my back for a moment. I didn't flinch or feel awkward. It felt right, like the hand of a relative I might have had.

"You holding up?" he asked.

I nodded, and smiled in a way that pressed my lips against my teeth, which helped me hold off the wave of tears I felt coming.

He took his hand back and set it in his lap. "I worked with your father at the plant." He said that this was before I was born. "I didn't even know that Lee had a son. I show up here, and there you are."

"I think I was a surprise for everyone," I said. "Even Mom and Dad."

He laughed. "Well, I'm sure a good one," he said, leaning back into the couch. "You know, I wanted to say something at the service today. That pastor said that anyone could come forward. I swear, I almost did, but I'm no public speaker. Not like you." He punched me lightly in the arm. "I liked that poem of yours."

"Thanks."

He told me that he wanted to tell me a story about Dad. "It's what I would have said at the service if I'd been brave enough to do it."

I turned to him. "I'd like to hear it," I said. I didn't know much about my dad's days at the plant.

Chuck told me that for a lot of years my dad was the shop steward on the floor for the union. "Real straight shooter," he said. "Always watching the company, making sure they were in compliance." He pointed his finger at the air in front of him. "Sometimes those stewards get a little too close to management and start thinking like them. Not your old man, though. He played by the book. A lot of the higher ups didn't like him because of it." Chuck laughed. "That's probably why we kept voting him into the position. He wasn't a pushover, though. He'd single out some of us guys and let us know when we were out of line, too. He was of the mind that one bad worker made all the workers look bad."

I nodded. It sounded like my dad.

Chuck explained that in the late Eighties, Dad was voted onto a bargaining team to negotiate a new contract. "You have to remember," he said, "this was when all kinds of plants were being shut down in Flint. There was this feeling of 'Hey, we're lucky to even have jobs' going through the rank and file. People were scared. Most of what we heard from management painted a pretty bleak outlook for the future."

He said that the bargaining team met with management, and it was some the fastest bargaining they'd ever seen. "So, the team comes back to the general assembly, and one after the other they started explaining the concessions we were going to have to take. 'Nature of the times' they kept saying." Chuck said that everybody in their seats just got really quiet and listened. A few people grumbled, but nobody openly protested. They already had

137

themselves ready for bad news. "It seemed like we were doing what we had to do. Then, your old man says that he'd like to say something. You could tell by the looks on the rest of the bargaining team's faces that they weren't expecting this. Your dad, he takes the mic and says that we should vote no on this contract. He says that we should send the team back in there to bargain in good faith. He says that he's ashamed of himself for not speaking up at the bargaining table. 'I'm new to this,' he says, 'but I've spent two sleepless nights thinking about it all, and I'm saying vote no. We're going to take some hits,' he says, 'but we don't have to give up all that they're asking. Sure, with everything going on, we're going to be screwed, but we don't have to hold our cheeks open and let them do it, right?'"

Chuck described how the whole place went crazy. "It was like your old man reached in and flipped a switch in their brains. About an hour later, they called for a vote. Over sixty percent voted no." Chuck sat up, took a pen from the coffee table, and started clicking it. "And, so, back to the table they went and came back with another version of the contract somewhat better than what they'd brought up the first time. And, again, just before the vote, your dad gets up and says a few things and has the whole room shouting again. Some were trying to shout him down. Others were shouting, 'Let him speak. Let him speak.' The bargaining team looked mad as hell." Chuck told me that a lot of the guys could see the writing on the wall. Dad was getting talked down around that bargaining table. He was outnumbered. Nobody saw things his way.

Chuck clicked the pen and looked at the tip sticking out like a little tongue. "That was his strategy. Come back to the hall and get all of us behind him. Get his voice heard where he could. And, so, that's what happened, a majority voted no again. I mean, most of us really trusted your old man. He had all those years of shop steward behind him. If something about the contract didn't look right to him, then something wasn't right."

Sitting there on that couch, he told me that the two teams went back to the table. "Three weeks," he said, "and they hammered out another contract." Then Chuck said something bad happened. Two nights before the contract was supposed to be presented to the rank and file, my dad was stopped by three guys outside of a bar. "Not to be ugly, but they beat the hell out of him...really bad. Broken ribs. Cracked jaw. Bruised kidneys. It was pretty obvious that somebody wanted him to shut the hell up." He explained that nobody ever learned the identity of the three guys. "The chances of it being random seemed pretty slim."

He set the pen down and rubbed his palms slowly together and nodded to himself. "There were all kinds of theories going around. Some said they were thugs hired by the company. Some said they were union guys who were afraid that ol' Lee Hoptner was going too far. Some said that it was union guys who wanted it to look like the company had done it, so your old man could be a martyr."

I sat. My face felt numb, tingly. "All I'd heard was that he'd taken early retirement," I said.

Chuck shrugged. "Well, he did. I don't blame him, either." He stood up. "I just wanted you to know that about your dad...that story. He did what he did, and it wasn't just for himself. Not everybody does things like that." He shook his head. "I really wish I would have said it at the service. I mean, it paints this picture of the kind of guy he was. Just didn't seem right, though...after your nice poem and everything. That story's got a lot of ugly in it. Plus, I just don't like to speak in front of people, you know?"

I nodded and thanked him for sharing the story with me.

After a few minutes, Chuck left. Others stopped to say their short goodbyes. The funeral director came by and told me that I could stay for as long as I needed. I sank back into the couch cushion. I tried to imagine my dad being jumped outside of a bar. For how much he loved history, he sure was reserved with sharing his own.

"What are you doing?"

I looked up at Heywood. "Just sitting here." From what I could see through doorways, most of the other lights in the building were off. "Probably time to get going."

He nodded. "You gonna fall out at my place again?"

I thought about it and then shook my head. "I think I'll give the house a try."

He reached a hand down to me and, when I took it, pulled me to my feet. "I'll follow you...just to get you settled in."

I didn't argue. I wasn't ready to be alone. Driving back to the house, I kept checking in the rearview mirror for his headlights behind me.

They were there.

Opening the front door, I stepped over a small pile of mail. The house smelled musty as it always did after being closed up for a few days. Heywood followed behind me into the kitchen. I asked him if he wanted a beer.

"I'm good," he said.

139

I leaned against the counter and looked out the sliding glass door into the dusk of the backyard. No ember. No small orange burning.

"I remember coming home after my brother passed," Heywood said. He was leaning against the entrance to the kitchen. "So much quiet like I was going deaf."

Dad was never loud, but he was always a steady series of sounds. A drill or hammer or lawn mowing or the scratch of shoveling or a ballgame on the radio. Hearing his noise, even if it were some faint scraping in the basement, was a way of knowing that I was home.

"It's so weird without him here." My last couple words broke at the end. During the previous days, I had thought about how I was alone in the world. It had just been a thought, a conclusion that I recognized and registered with a sentence in my head. "I am alone," I had thought. Coming home to that cellar-quiet house, though...that was different. I wasn't thinking about my loneliness, I was feeling it.

Heywood put his arms around me and held me in a long hug. His hand rubbed my shoulder. "It's going to be alright, brother."

I was crying. No sound, just tears breaking over the rim of my lower lids and streaking down my cheeks. Even though I tried to fight them, I exhaled a few blubbery sobs.

"It's good, D. Gotta let that out."

When he released me after a minute, I did feel better. I was less bound, less constricted. I felt the way that I might finally sleep a real sleep after two nights of restlessness on Heywood's floor.

"You gonna be aight?"

I nodded. "I think so."

"You sure?" He told me he'd sleep on the couch if that's what I wanted.

"No, man, I'll be good. Need to get used to it anyway, right?"

Opening the door, he turned around and pointed at me. "Hey, no work for this home skillet tomorrow. I'll holla at ya."

I smiled and nodded. "That'd be good."

The sputtering noise of his exhaust manifold faded down the street. I knelt to the pile of mail and began to sort it into bills and what looked like junk mail. There was still so much to do with the probate court to get Dad's affairs in order.

Lee Hoptner.

It was strange to see his name on envelopes again and again.

Sifting, I found a letter addressed to me. I looked at the return address.

Hartland Insurance.

Opening it, I expected to find a check, a somewhat good end to the day. I looked through the envelope a couple times before reading the single-paragraph letter that was enclosed.

Dear Mr. Denver Hoptner:

Your contact information was found among Mr. Wallace's personal belongings. It may be that you are awaiting some kind of correspondence from him regarding important matters to you. We felt it incumbent upon the company to contact you to let you know that Mr. Wallace suffered a cerebrovascular accident upon his return from the Saginaw conference. We await, yet, the doctor's full prognosis. We know only that if there is to be a recovery, it will be long and difficult.

If the business that you had with Mr. Wallace can be handled through personnel within the company, please do not hesitate to reach us with the contact information provided below.

I slumped against the door, staring at my finger where the ring my father had picked out for me had been. Saginaw had stolen it. The skin there was pale and sickly looking.

16.

A big wind came and swept my stack of 500 fliers off the porch and over the front yard, the street, and the yards on the other side of Gratiot. I stood for a moment with an electrical plug in my hand, watching the sheets blowing and drifting like so much snow.

That morning, I'd stopped by Bruce's coffee shop to pick up my amp and microphone. I was ready for him to be confrontational. Instead, he showed me where he kept them, helped me carry them out to the truck, and even shook my hand. It was like we were old friends.

I crouched and plugged the amplifier into an outlet I found out on the porch. Holding the microphone, I stood up and looked out at Gratiot. The morning commuters on their way to work slowed and drove cautiously through all that paper. Maybe the wind had been a blessing. Some had their windows open. I shouted into the microphone: "Save this house! Save this house!" I had a bucket down by the sidewalk with a sign marked "Donations."

I was only at it for about twenty-five minutes when I looked out and saw a police car trying to turn left into the Roethke two-rut driveway. The traffic in the other lane inching through the sea of papers was keeping the officer from making his turn.

I should have been nervous, afraid. Instead I felt clear. Maybe it was the clarity of sleeplessness. I didn't go to sleep after reading the letter about D.W. Wallace's condition. I researched on the Internet. A cerebrovascular accident meant that Mr. Wallace had suffered a stroke. Minor or major, he had a long recovery ahead of him—a recovery that probably wouldn't include him worrying too much about the Roethke House. Lying in bed, staring up into the darkness of the ceiling, I realized what I had to do. I spent hours on a flier that described why the Roethke House should mean something to Saginaw and why people should donate. The writing wasn't too bad. I printed copies from my computer until there was no paper left in the house. At six thirty I drove to Bruce's shop for my equipment.

The officer pulled up into the yard. By that time, I was already on the roofers' extension ladder, the rungs cold against my palms, climbing it like a cat going up a curtain. I stopped halfway, cupped a hand to my mouth, and shouted, "Save this house!" A puzzled driver looked my way. Getting to the top, I stepped off the ladder and onto the roof. The shingles were like sandpaper under my feet. Grabbing either side, I tipped the ladder backwards, and it clattered into a scraggily hedge not far from where the officer was standing looking up at me. He picked a CB from his shoulder and spoke something into it that I couldn't hear. I looked over the roofs and tree tops of Saginaw. The branches were bucking like horses, just like Roethke had said. In the distance, the buildings of the downtown glowed in the rising sun. Everything was leaves and concrete and cloud-smoked blue sky. You wouldn't have known there could be so much beauty in this place.

The slope of the roof was steep. Tiny granules broke loose under my feet and spilled down into the gutter. I steadied my hand on the attic dormer and thought of my father. I only knew that it was called a dormer because of him. I cupped both hands around my mouth and shouted toward the street. "Save this house!"

I might have been crying.

The officer yelled something up toward me. I couldn't hear anything in the wind. A few people stopped along the sidewalk to gawk. I shouted, "Save this house!"

A man on the sidewalk gestured toward his ear and shook his head. One of my fliers was on his foot. I pointed, but he didn't seem to know what I meant. I shouted again to the small crowd.

Another police car pulled up onto the lawn. Then a news van. Two officers ran out of the car and toward the other officer and the ladder. I thought of *Alice in Wonderland* when the White Rabbit's men were trying to get the giant Alice out of the rabbit's house. She snatched her big fingers out the window, knocking them shattering into the cucumber frames. Or, using her foot she kicked one of them right back up the chimney. "There goes Bill!" I smiled, imagining the anthropomorphic lizard sailing through the air.

My mind was really exhausted…gone.

The top part of the ladder banged against the gutter. More people had gathered on the sidewalk. They were pointing. I looked into the face of an older black woman. She was worrying a chain with a crucifix on it through her fingers. She mouthed "Don't jump" to me.

"Save this house!" I shouted.

"All right, let's get you down, now."

I turned. An officer was coming up over the roof's edge. He was holding a palm out toward me. "Take it easy."

Gripping the dormer's edge, I made my way toward the other side of the roof.

"Just come with me," he said, finding his balance. "You're not in trouble."

I looked. Not far away was the chimney. On the ground, a reporter was standing with a microphone, her back to the house. Her cameraman was crouching. When he rose to standing, he was holding one of my fliers.

The officer was on the other side of the dormer. I looked into his concerned eyes.

"My father died," I said, wiping tears.

"It's okay." He reached out toward me. "I'll get you over to the ladder. It'll be okay."

I let go, started for the chimney, and then turned back toward the officer. His hand was stretching for me. I nodded, going toward him. Then a gust of wind ripped through. Something happened with my balance. My feet slid. The officer's face changed and let me know that I was falling. The side of my ribs banged against the roof, knocking the wind from me. I rolled, trying to get my fingers over the edge of the gutter. A second later, my back and elbow crashed into the roof of the porch.

I rolled again, over the edge, and toward the yard...plummeting.

17.

I turned on the television and then, feeling guilty, turned it off again. There were pieces of paper on the tray in front of me. A few were balled up. Most were filled with lines that I'd crossed out. I had a new blank piece of paper. I set the tip of my pen down and dragged it back and forth slowly but with increasing force until I'd gouged through the paper, the paper beneath it, and into the surface of the tray. A shot of pain went through my torso like lightning.

The first fall down to the porch roof shattered my elbow, bruised a kidney, and broke a rib. When I went from the porch to the lawn, I fractured my right knee, broke two more ribs, and knocked out a tooth. The doctor said that it could have been a lot worse, especially if I'd fallen straight to the ground from the roof.

My door opened and the day nurse came in. She asked how I was feeling and if I needed anything.

"I think I'm good," I said.

She pointed to a Percocet tablet on my nightstand. "You didn't take it."

I lied and told her that I wasn't feeling any discomfort, even though my elbow felt like I was nesting it in a bed of hot coals.

She picked up the pill in one hand and my Styrofoam cup of ice water in the other. "You should take it now," she said. "You don't want the pain to sneak up on you."

I took the pill from her and set it in my mouth. She tilted the straw toward me, and I took a sip.

"We have to stay on the schedule, or you'll be dealing with some serious pain."

After she left, I slipped the tablet out from under my tongue and put it back on the nightstand. I wanted to stay clear, at least for a while longer. I set another fresh piece of paper on top of the piece that I'd just destroyed.

It hadn't been more than an hour since Vance had stopped in to see me. He'd told me that Ricky was out in the hallway trying to get up the courage to come in. "He says people in hospital beds give him the creeps."

I laughed. "So he's just standing out there?"

"He's texting."

We both laughed.

Vance stayed only for a few minutes. Before he left, he handed me a folded up piece of paper. "One of my hunting poems," he said. "Don't read it until I leave. It's probably pretty bad."

Ricky came in about a minute after Vance left. I heard Vance telling him to get his ass in there and say something.

Ricky paced around the room and only managed sidelong glances. "Man, you're fucking crazy, College. What the hell were you thinking?" He shook his head. "Never would have guessed it. I was working with a nutcase." He stopped and looked at me full on for the first time. "Just had to be on television, didn't you?" He smiled. "You're a piece of fucking work."

I shrugged my right shoulder.

Standing in the doorway, he told me to get better. Then he leaned in toward the bed and lowered his voice to just above a whisper. "If you don't use all the pain killers that they send you home with, let me know. I know somebody that will buy them." He nodded and made an affirming noise in his throat. "I'll split the money with you."

The camera guy from the news crew had caught my fall off of the Roethke roof. The reporter read my flier. Following up, they tracked down and interviewed Abby Waters. Five hours later, they'd edited together a unique story for their six o'clock newscast. It was the kind of oddball piece that the national news stations sometimes pick up for broadcast, which was exactly what happened.

I had a phone call from Abby the second day I was in the hospital. I was a little out of it from the Percocet, but understood the gist of what she was saying. Apparently many people had seen the newscast. She'd received dozens of emails and phone calls promising that donations were on the way. An eighty-four-year-old woman who had married very well said that a check for two thousand dollars was in the mail. She'd been a student of Roethke's at Bennington. "We've already received over three thousand from local donors alone," Abby told me.

I looked at my attempts at a poem. They were garbage. Then, I opened Vance's poem and read it again:

Thanksgiving Eve

We gather here this night
at our fire
We eat our small meal and have our small drink

146

as the snow lazily falls like crystals from the sky
We talk of seasons past
against a lean-to
We enjoy the night
We play music softly
Play softly as the snow falls
The snowflakes dance with the music
We bed down for the night in peace
Tomorrow when sun makes daylight
we become predators once again
searching for the kill
in this beautiful land we call home

I read it a couple more times. I could see Vance out there in the coming-winter weather with his family. I could feel their closeness and the splendor of the night. I liked the repetition of the word "softly" and how the "sun makes daylight." I liked the mix of softness with the unexpected hardness in the last lines. I liked that it was Vance. No concerns about who might say what in workshop or what magazine might be interested in publishing it. It wasn't just pure sentiment either. It was about people and how we can be gentle in one moment and killers in the next…without such a message ever being Vance's intention. It was pure.

I looked at the blank piece of paper on my tray and shook my head. Touching the remote, I turned on the television and closed my eyes. The Tigers were on. It sounded like they were winning. The commentators made it sound as though they didn't have much of a chance at the playoffs. "Still," one said, "some of these rookies are showing a lot of promise, especially since the All-Star game. Next year we could be looking at a really solid team thanks to all this young blood. They're bringing some really good spirit to the ball club."

Someone knocked on the door. I opened my dozing eyes to Heywood in the doorway.

"Nurse said you were awake."

"I am," I said, smiling through the pain. The television was on a commercial. I shut it off.

Heywood walked over to the bedside table and dropped a couple envelopes on it. He'd been bringing my mail for the past few days.

"You okay, man? You're whiter than usual."

I pulled a few tissues from my box and mopped them across my forehead. The pain felt like it had its own pulse. "I'm alright."

147

He nodded, then dropped down into the visitor chair.

I adjusted myself on the bed, and the pain closed my eyes. Black dots floated across the pink of my eyelids. I heard myself make a noise.

"Want me to get the nurse?"

I shook my head. Reaching for it, I popped the Percocet and swallowed it with a mouthful of water. "Just time for my meds. I'll be alright once they kick in." There'd be no writing for me.

He looked at me, shaking his head. "Say the word and I'll jet."

"No, I'll be fine. Just knowing that the good stuff is in my system already has me feeling better." Like the doctor told me to, I imagined the pill breaking up in the digestive fluids, the oxycodone getting into my blood. He'd said that visualizing could make the relief come that much faster. "What's new with you, anyway?" I asked.

He reached into his front pocket, pulled out a folded piece a paper, and flipped it up onto my chest.

I picked it up with my good hand and waved it open. It was an acceptance letter from *Rattle* magazine. I looked at him and smiled. "You're going to have a poem published."

He shrugged. "Looks that way."

"Shit, man, that's great. That's really great." I didn't feel any of the old jealousies. I was really happy for him. Really. "*Rattle*'s a good mag," I said.

He got up and took the letter. "No big thing," he said, folding it back into his pocket and sitting down.

"No, it is a big thing. I went to school with people who couldn't get a poem in *Rattle*. Hell, I couldn't."

Heywood smiled and scratched his forehead. "Pretty big thing at the house. Ma dukes is taking me to dinner tonight. I think she's even paying, which means we probably splitting an extra value meal but, still, she's really buggin' about the whole thing."

"She should be, man. I mean, shit, congratulations."

He nodded and couldn't keep from really smiling. "Thanks, D."

I rested my head against the pillow and closed my eyes. I really had put off the Percocet way too long.

"What's on the paper?" he asked, pointing.

I kept my eyes closed. "Nothing."

I heard him stand up and get closer to the bed. "Looks like you're working on a poem."

I opened my eyes, looked at the paper, and then closed them again. "Nope. I'm just practicing crossing out every piece of shit word I write. I'm getting good at it."

He sat. "Keep going. You'll get it."

"You know, I used to think that it was lack of experience that kept me from writing anything good. Now, I've had all this stuff go down, and I can't write a word about it."

"It's too early…everything's still too raw. Lying here all bum rushed. That's no time to work on a poem."

Another wave of pain went through me, blocking out everything else. I didn't know how long it was before I spoke again. "I don't know, man," I said, almost whispering. "Maybe I'm not a poet. Maybe I never will be."

After a few seconds of silence, I could hear Heywood laughing. I opened my eyes. "What?"

"Shit, man, you fuckin' serious? A poem? What the hell you care about writing some poem?" He stood up and pointed at me. "You are a fuckin' poem, D."

"What are you—"

"You did some big shit, man. Big. Feel good about that for awhile. Poems…they just the wish, just the symbol of what we want to be. They just a way of looking at things. You, man…you did something. You saved that fuckin' house. You made the symbol real. You the thing people write poems about." He laughed and shook his head. "Look, D…you got me talking college like you."

I lay there trying to let myself feel good the way Heywood said I should.

Before he left he told me he'd be by again the next day. "You probably won't know it, but I'll be here."

I was scheduled to have surgery on my arm the next day. The doctor had explained about the titanium plate and the screws and pin that would hold the pieces of my elbow together. Of all my injuries, it was going to require the longest recovery time. I closed my eyes. It felt like the Percocet was working. The pain was down to a simmer.

Heather had called me the night before having seen the news story. She told me how sorry she was to hear about my father. We talked for almost an hour. She told me that she was going to drive up and see me after my surgery. She explained that she'd taken an assistantship to go to Western Michigan University to work on a PhD. in Creative Writing.

"I did research," she said. "People with PhDs are edging out people with MFAs for jobs. It's really competitive."

"Sounds like a smart choice," I said, hearing myself sounding like my father.

"Western is closer to my parents, too," she said.

"Not that far from Saginaw, either," I said.

"I know."

Maybe it was just the pain meds, but the way we talked...I don't know. It felt like there was still something there. I looked forward to finding out.

I planned to sell the house. Dad had quite a bit of debt from Mom's treatment, more than he let on. The sale of the house would let me pay that off. It would also leave me with some money to live on for awhile. I'd heard from one of the nurses that I could substitute teach with my bachelor's degree. Felt like something I should try once I was on my feet again.

I yawned. The Percocet was really starting to kick in

I turned the television back on. The Tigers were still ahead by two runs. I watched for a few innings, and the commentator was right. The rookies were good. Really good. They'd make all the difference in the years ahead.

I drifted down into sleep and dreams...

I was walking with the descendents of Raven's Eye. They told me that some of the Sauks had escaped...had run off into the forest during the attack. They'd gone into hiding. I was speaking with the great-great-great-great grandsons and daughters of the survivors. They said they lived for centuries in the patches of forest that remained. "Hiding was not difficult," the chief said. "So few go into the trees since the lumberjacks." In the dream, I could understand Algonquin. We were walking through the wreckage of Saginaw's deserted neighborhood streets. The houses around us were gutted, without doors or glass in the windows.

d.a. levy was there with us wearing his jean jacket and sunglasses. He had a scraggily beard. "i want to watch what you cats do here," he said. "if it works, i'll bring this shit back to cleveland with me."

Roethke was there, too, shambling behind us in a suit and long, black overcoat.

Above us, small birds flew from the windows of the empty buildings.

"i've never heard that bird before," levy said.

Roethke, speaking for the first time, identified it: "It's a vireo's warbling." While we walked, he talked at great length about many different birds. His voice was childlike and excited. Then, he suddenly stopped. Standing in the street, he shadow boxed.

levy urged him to keep talking, but he wouldn't.

Our pilgrimage passed through the dead streets of the downtown. There were no other people. It was then that I noticed all the rabbits following us at a distance.

We soon came to the river's edge.

"Here," the chief said. The others began to clear away the debris and refuse of hundreds of years.

Ievy sat on the hood of an abandoned car and watched.

The chief looked at the concrete and rust with faraway eyes. "Is this why they had wanted it so badly?"

I walked down to the water.

Roethke was in the shallows with his pants rolled up to his knees. His coat was on the shore. Standing among sunken bottles and pebbles, the image of his feet wavered beneath the surface. He looked at me. "I knew this place as a boy," he said, turning back to the river. "I've carried it like a father's ghost."

Behind me, the Sauks crouched to plant corn in the space they'd cleared. Their regal mohawks were like manes. The rabbits nibbled at grasses growing in the cracked asphalt of a nearby parking lot. Standing to stretch his back, one of the small tribe motioned for me to come help.

I went to them, eager to plant. I found my parents crouched among them. My mother smiled up at me from where she knelt with her fingers in the earth. "I knew you'd pitch in," my father said.

The soft bells of the winter pony chimed in the air all around us.

Roethke was still in the water looking at his feet in the bed of the river. He fished a scrap of paper and a stub of pencil from his pant pocket and scribbled something down.

Ievy looked at me and smiled. Then he pointed a finger gun at his forehead and fired his thumb.

I wrenched my eyes awake. It was dark outside the hospital window. Someone walked by out in the hallway. Then it was quiet again. I had no pain.

The doctor had told me that the Percocet might cause vivid and strange dreams. He wasn't kidding.

In the dream—seeing my parents—it had seemed so real. They were gone, though. I'd never see them again. The wet warmth of my tears slid down my cheeks. They were both buried out at Oakwood Cemetery, not all that far from Roethke's grave.

The backside of the Beans Bunny glowed atop the grain elevator roof in the night sky's distance. I thought— really for the first time—about what I'd done at the Roethke House. Like Heywood

151

had suggested, I let myself feel good about it, let it wash over and through me. It was something…something real and good. Probably the biggest thing I'd ever done.

Like Heather's poem said, God was in what I'd done. God was in Helen placing twenty dollars in my palm. God was in the movement of my fingers typing up the flier. God was in the wind and in my slipping.

The fall, too. God was in my fall.

God wouldn't be in the poem that I would probably never write, anyway. The poem and not writing it didn't matter.

I lay there looking out at that long-eared neon glowing in all that blackness. I should have been in pain, should have been hurting. I felt nothing but good.

I knew my injuries. Not only had the doctor explained them, but I'd heard them listed on one of the national newscasts. I slid my tongue up into the smooth space where my tooth had been.

My father had said that there were many years that the Beans Bunny wasn't lit. There just wasn't money. Then a fund raising effort was started by a local history buff. They sold stuffed animal bunnies every year and raised enough to keep the sign maintained. I remember my dad pointing his finger at me when he said, "That's the largest figural neon sign in the United States." He looked back at it as we drove past on I-675. "It's been damaged by ice and struck by lightning. Lots a reasons to just let the damn thing go black. Still," he said, "a handful of people keep it going—keep it lit."

A flickering pink rabbit perched over a city of wolves. A beacon…a rabbit over Saginaw. I smiled, imagining what d.a. levy might have said if he saw it:

"it's a start, man. it's a fuckin' start."

152

ABOUT THE AUTHOR:

Jeff Vande Zande began to write as a poet in reaction to his father who was a fiction writer. "It was a rebellion of sorts," he says. Some of his poems were nominated for Pushcart Prizes, and one of them was selected to appear in Ted Kooser's syndicated newspaper column, *American Life in Poetry*. His poems from chapbooks were eventually collected in a book, *Poems New, Used, and Rebuilds* (March Street Press). Vande Zande began writing short stories seriously in 1997 and focused more on his fiction after that. "More and more, the world came to me as stories rather than poems," he says. Bottom Dog Press has published his *Emergency Stopping and Other Stories* (2004) and his novel, *Landscape with Fragmented Figures* (2009). Additionally, he has published a novella collected with five stories, *Threatened Species* (Whistling Shade Press, 2010). The author has taught for the last ten years at Delta College, a community college in Michigan that serves the cities of Midland, Bay City, and Saginaw. *American Poet* comes out of his experience as a poet, as a teacher, and as a transplanted advocate of Saginaw, declaring it, "a city with a rich history that includes struggle, but also the seeds of its rebirth."

Although much of *American Poet* is fiction, poet Theodore Roethke was indeed born and raised in Saginaw. His boyhood home is still there on Gratiot St. with his uncle's regal fieldstone home next door. A very real organization, the Friends of Theodore Roethke Foundation works to preserve the home and is trying to grow it into a museum, writers retreat, and community outreach center. You can find out more about them and their need for your financial support at www.roethkehouse.org.

Vande Zande maintains a website at www.jeffvandezande.com.

OTHER BOOKS BY
BIRD DOG PUBLISHING

A Poetic Journey: Poems
by Robert A. Reynolds, 86 pgs. $16
Dogs and Other Poems
by Paul Piper, 80 pgs. $15
The Mermaid Translation
by Allen Frost, 140 pgs. $15
Heart Murmurs: Poems
by John Vanek, 120 pgs. $15
Home Recordings: Tales and Poems
by Allen Frost. $14
A Life in Poems
by William C. Wright, $10
Faces and Voices: Tales
by Larry Smith, 136 pgs. $14
Second Story Woman: A Memoir of Second Chances
by Carole Calladine, 226 pgs. $15
256 Zones of Gray: Poems
by Rob Smith, 80 pgs. $14
Another Life: Collected Poems
by Allen Frost, 176 pgs. $14
Winter Apples: Poems
by Paul S. Piper, 88 pgs. $14
Lake Effect: Poems
by Laura Treacy Bentley, 108 pgs. $14
Depression Days on an Appalachian Farm: Poems
by Robert L. Tener, 80 pgs. $14
120 Charles Street, The Village: Journals & Other Writings 1949-1950
by Holly Beye, 240 pgs. $15

BIRD DOG PUBLISHING
A division of Bottom Dog Press, Inc.
Order Online at:
http://smithdocs.net/BirdDogy/BirdDogPage.html